Why had he brought her home?

He'd known it was a mistake. It was just that for a second he'd been overcome by a protective streak he couldn't explain, one he didn't even like. Rescuing women was a fool's errand—he'd done it once, and he wasn't going to do it again. He glanced back at Megan, and the memory of holding her swamped him—the soft, yielding quality of her body, the smell of her hair. She was so beautiful. Was that it?

No, it wasn't just her current vulnerability that attracted him. It wasn't just her big blue eyes or her body, either. Those things were distractions, sure, but distractions that were relatively easy to dismiss. After all, there were lots of pretty and needy women in the world.

What Megan possessed was far more dangerous. To his resolve. To his heart.

But he couldn't seem to stop thinking about her …

Dear Reader,

Traditionally June is the month for weddings, so Silhouette Romance cordially invites you to enjoy our promotion JUNE BRIDES, starting with Suzanne Carey's *Sweet Bride of Revenge*. In this sensuously powerful VIRGIN BRIDES tale, a man forces the daughter of his nemesis to marry him, never counting on falling in love with the enemy....

Up-and-comer Robin Nicholas delivers a touching BUNDLES OF JOY titled *Man, Wife and Little Wonder*. Can a denim-clad, Harley-riding bad boy turn doting dad and dedicated husband? Find out in this classic marriage-of-convenience romance! Next, Donna Clayton's delightful duo MOTHER & CHILD continues with the evocative title *Who's the Father of Jenny's Baby?* A woman awakens in the hospital to discover she has amnesia—and she's pregnant! Problem is, *two* men claim to be the baby's father—her estranged husband...and her husband's brother!

Granted: Wild West Bride is the next installment in Carol Grace's BEST-KEPT WISHES series. This richly Western romance pairs a toughened, taut-muscled cowboy and a sophisticated city gal who welcomes his kisses, but will she accept his ring? For a fresh spin on the bridal theme, try Alice Sharpe's *Wife on His Doorstep*. An about-to-be bride stops her wedding to the wrong man, only to land on the doorstep of the strong, silent ship captain who was to perform the ill-fated nuptials.... And in Leanna Wilson's latest Romance, *His Tomboy Bride*, Nick Latham was *supposed* to "give away" childhood friend and bride-to-be Billie Rae—not claim the transformed beauty as his own!

We hope you enjoy the month's wedding fun, and return each and every month for more classic, emotional, heartwarming novels from Silhouette Romance.

Enjoy!

Joan Marlow Golan

Joan Marlow Golan
Senior Editor Silhouette Romance

Please address questions and book requests to:
Silhouette Reader Service
U.S.: 3010 Walden Ave., P.O. Box 1325, Buffalo, NY 14269
Canadian: P.O. Box 609, Fort Erie, Ont. L2A 5X3

WIFE ON HIS DOORSTEP

Alice Sharpe

Silhouette
ROMANCE™
Published by Silhouette Books
America's Publisher of Contemporary Romance

This book is dedicated to Barbara Brett and Marcia Book Adirim, whom I have been fortunate enough to count as both editors and friends.

A special thanks to Captain Dennis Moore and the crew of the sternwheeler Columbia Gorge, who I hope will forgive me for taking a few small liberties with their ship.

 SILHOUETTE BOOKS

ISBN 0-373-19304-1

WIFE ON HIS DOORSTEP

Printed in U.S.A.

Books by Alice Sharpe

Silhouette Romance

Going to the Chapel #1137
Missing: One Bride #1212
Wife on His Doorstep #1304

Silhouette Yours Truly

If Wishes Were Heroes

ALICE SHARPE

met her husband-to-be on a cold, foggy beach in Northern California. One year later they were married. Their union has survived the rearing of two children, a handful of earthquakes registering over 6.5, numerous cats and a few special dogs, the latest of which is a yellow Lab named Annie Rose. Alice and her husband now live in a small rural town in Oregon, where she devotes the majority of her time to pursuing her second love, writing.

WELCOME TO OREGON

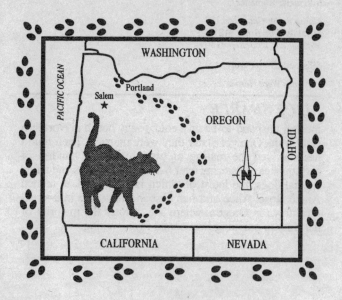

HOME OF FOGGY DEW

Chapter One

John Vermont, owner and acting captain of the stern-wheeler *Ruby Rose,* didn't like marrying people. For one thing, seeing as he currently spent most of his time ashore, he was sorely out of practice, which meant that instead of reciting the vows in his deep baritone—which could, when he wanted, scare an oyster off a rock—he had to read them from the manual. For another, face it, he didn't really believe in marriage—personal experience had taught him the term "wedded bliss" was an oxymoron.

Take the couple standing in front of him now. Within the next few minutes John would pronounce them husband and wife, yet he couldn't help but wonder if they had any idea what they were getting into.

The groom was a man about his own age, sporting an out-of-season tan and a twelve-hundred-dollar tuxedo. Earlier, before the ceremony, John had seen the guy strutting around the deck, acting like he owned the boat, a crowd of cronies following in his wake, laughing at his jokes, smiling into his eyes while he puffed out his chest and ate it up.

The bride was a good five or six years younger than the groom—still in her twenties. She had sassy blond hair cut short around her ears, a lithe figure, and huge blue eyes filled with doubts. She used those eyes to cast furtive glances at the man she was marrying, glances of which the groom seemed totally unaware, glances that seemed to say "Just a second, let me rethink this!"

Made you wonder why she was marrying him.

Judging from what John had heard, money was the likely answer. Mrs. Colpepper, the new events coordinator John had hired after the old one ran away with the then-acting captain of this boat, had mentioned that the groom was footing the bill for the wedding. Lobster and champagne for one hundred and fifty didn't come cheaply. Nor did the well-known band tuning up its instruments on the lower deck or the hundreds of flowers fluttering their petals in the freshening breeze.

Just another pretty woman marrying another rich clown for all the wrong reasons. Boy, did that bring back the memories!

Running a finger down the page, John discovered it was time to remind everyone that marriage was not an institution to be entered into lightly. How was that for a novel idea? The bride bit her lip as he spoke and, raising her eyes, she gazed at him. He almost felt as though he should pause to reassure her, but he wasn't the reassuring kind. At six-three and one hundred and ninety solid pounds, he was too big; his features, though regular enough, were too weathered by his predilection for the outdoors, his manner too brusque. Women tended to find him threatening. Truth of the matter was, the feeling was entirely mutual.

He cast out the next line, giving it all he had. "If there is anyone here who knows of a reason why these two shouldn't be married, let him speak now or forever hold his peace."

In the bottom of his black little heart, he always kind

of hoped *someone* would come forward at this point—it would at least break the monotony. As usual, however, no one did.

Correction: no *person* did. Foggy Dew, the ship's cat, made a sudden appearance. John had taken pity on her when he'd come aboard less than a month before and found her on the dock, knocked up and abandoned. She'd repaid him by shedding on his clothes, sleeping on his bunk and, generally speaking, taking over the ship. Now, as he watched, she waddled deliberately around and about the chairs filled with prosperous-looking wedding guests, steering clear of Mrs. Colpepper, who had forcefully declared her dislike of cats, pregnant ones in particular.

Like a good captain, he struggled to keep his mind on the ceremony, though he was aware the cat had paused between the bridal couple to sniff at the hem of the woman's dress. She glanced down at Foggy Dew, her features relaxing perceptibly. The cat meowed, and a smile— the first John had seen—touched the bride's lips, lit her eyes and transformed her face from simple beauty to breath-stopping perfection.

For no clear reason John suddenly found his tongue getting in the way of the words, a condition he quickly remedied with a stern clearing of his throat. As he continued, he noted that Foggy Dew, having conquered the bride, had moved on to inspect the groom, who cast a scowl at the cat and then at John. With a nonchalant shrug, John tried to say, "Lighten up, mister, she'll go away in a second."

The groom didn't seem to get the message. He tried scooting Foggy Dew away with a stiff leg, but perversely, this seemed to make the cat even more determined to win his affection. Purring loudly now, she rubbed her chin along the man's shoe. John could feel Mrs. Colpepper's gaze drilling holes in his head as she waited for him to make the cat cease and desist, but doing that would mean stopping the ceremony and that might mean starting over again at the beginning. This was out of the question seeing as he was almost at the end. So he did the only thing he could think to do—he spoke faster.

Besides, the episode was not without a lighter side. Take the bride, for instance. She'd stopped looking uneasy and was instead smiling at the cat, a definite improvement. Even the guests, stuffed shirts that most of them seemed to be, were smiling at the incongruity of a cat aboard a boat inviting itself to a wedding. Heck, the kid recording the ceremony for posterity was grinning, too. Chances were someday this obnoxious groom would look at the video and think a cat showing up was kind of cute.

John moved on to the next part, fighting to place a solemn yet serene look upon his face. The vows, all those little words and repetitions that promised love and fidelity, sometimes stuck in his throat.

As the bride said her lines, she looked him straight in the eye. Normally, in his experience, a woman looked at her husband-to-be at a time like this and not at the captain of the vessel. He glanced down at the manual to find her name, which Mrs. Colpepper had penciled in the margin, then he looked back at her. "Do you, Megan Ashley Morison—" he began. The use of her name seemed to shake her, as though until that second she'd been kidding herself into thinking it was someone else standing at this seaboard altar, someone else promising to cleave herself only unto the groom.

In fact, her demeanor was so unusual that by the time she whispered, "I do," John was surprised—and oddly disappointed—she'd gone through with it.

Now it was time to address the groom, one Robert Winslow, who was still fidgeting because of the cat. As John asked him to repeat his vows, Foggy Dew finally gave up and settled down into a lumpy mass of fur at the guy's feet, so it was hard to figure why instead of just saying "I do'' and moving away, Winslow chose that second to act. With a sneer and a grunt, the man kicked the cat.

John watched in stunned silence as a gray blur of fur, two wild yellow eyes, and twenty extended claws hurled toward him, and though he quickly knelt to intercept her, he was too late. She flew between the railing and the deck and landed with a splash in the river twenty feet below.

Almost immediately, the bride was at the rail, her bouquet of roses and lilies dropped in haste. John, at the rail seconds before her, was marking the animal's location by lining her up with an outcrop of rock on the shoreline when Megan Morison grabbed his arm. "What can I do?"

The hush that had at first descended was suddenly filled with shocked voices, including Mrs. Colpepper's, who was demanding the ceremony continue.

John took Megan's hand and pulled her away from the rail. "Come with me."

"Now wait just a second—" Winslow began, but by then John was racing toward the stairs leading down, Megan's hand still in his. On the lower deck, which was decorated to the hilt but devoid of passengers except for the band and the ship's caterers who were setting up for the reception, he released Megan and pulled a life ring with an attached line from a bulkhead.

As he slid aside the door, which opened close to the water, Megan rushed past him. He grabbed her arm, sure for a second she was going to trip on her long dress and take a dive. She glanced up at him. "I'm okay," she said.

"Passengers in the water give my insurance adjuster hives. Do you see the cat?"

Together, they scanned the choppy surface of the river. Thankfully they were anchored in a small, calm bight with little or no current but though John easily found the rocks on the shoreline, the cat, similar in color to the gray water, had disappeared. For one long moment, he thought she'd drowned.

Megan was standing so close to him that he felt her body tense as she threw out an arm. "There she is, over there!"

John followed her pointing finger until he made out Foggy Dew's small head and paws, which were slashing frantically at the water.

"Don't let her out of your sight," he said.

"Just hurry."

John threw the life ring beyond the cat. As he steadily pulled it toward the frightened animal, he was aware of voices and then of people crowding the lower deck. He tuned them out, directing all his concentration toward reaching the cat in time.

When the life ring loomed by Foggy Dew's side, she gave it two looks. The first seemed to say, "What in the world is that thing?" The second one was just as clear. "Whatever it is, it's better than the water." With determination, she hooked a few claws into the ring and attempted to climb to dry land.

John very gently tugged the ring toward the boat. Over his shoulder, he recognized Winslow's voice as he snarled, "That damn cat got exactly what it deserved." The life ring was very close now and John looked over his shoulder to find Megan. He wanted her to hold on to the line as he retrieved the cat.

As he turned, the groom flew past him. With a splash, the idiot landed in the river, his wake pushing the life ring away. Megan, who was staring down at her soon-to-be husband, was white with fury or concern—it was hard to tell which. Mrs. Colpepper screamed, a few of the wedding guests gasped, and John was relieved to see Foggy Dew had held on.

Now he had two passengers overboard, but it never entered his mind to rescue the man before the cat. The fool had jumped in, let him paddle around out there for a second or two—it wouldn't kill him. Foggy Dew was bursting with unborn kittens.

Mrs. Colpepper appeared at his side. "I demand you pull Mr. Winslow out of the water at once!" she sputtered.

Ignoring her, John found Megan's hand. "Hold this," he said as he pushed the line into her hand. He then dropped to the deck, flattened himself out on his stomach and, reaching down, snagged Foggy Dew by the scruff of her neck, lifting her aboard as he stood.

Without hesitation, Megan reached out and took the wild-eyed, sopping-wet cat, who responded to a stranger with a yowl and a manic attempt to escape. Several long red slashes popped out on Megan's arm as she subdued the animal and folded it within the lacy bulk of her pristine wedding gown.

"Captain Vermont, this is absolutely outrageous," Mrs. Colpepper screeched. "I won't stand for this. I simply won't!"

"Robert doesn't swim," an older woman cried. She looked enough like the groom to be his mother, and John turned back to the water. Sure enough, Winslow seemed to be having a difficult time. John quickly cast the life ring out to the man, who looped an arm over it and waited to be hauled aboard.

Jeez, would it kill the S.O.B. to paddle some?

"If Robert doesn't swim," John said with conviction as he heaved on the line, "why in blazes did he jump in the river? If he was sorry for kicking my cat, a simple apology would have sufficed. He very nearly made matters worse."

"But he didn't jump!" Mrs. Colpepper squealed.

"*She* pushed him!" the mother yelped, pointing an accusing finger at Megan.

While John pulled Robert Winslow toward the boat, he looked down at the woman who cradled his cat. She met his gaze with a defiant look, the intensity of which was hampered only slightly by the bright pink flush that suffused her neck and face and the trembling of her beautiful lips.

"Did you?"

She nodded.

He decided discretion was called for, so he put off thanking her until later. Instead he turned to the river and, along with a couple of the groom's men, hauled the man back aboard the *Ruby Rose.*

Some of the cockiness had been washed away by the cold, clean water, but John knew men like this, and he knew recovery would be swift and sure. Standing on the deck surrounded by friends and family, with water running down his face and dripping puddles around his patent-leather shoes, Winslow still managed to look in control, even with his tuxedo plastered against his sturdy body.

"What in the world did you do that for?" Winslow snarled at Megan.

Hugging the wad of the top layer of her skirt—which presumably held Foggy Dew—close to her chest, she met his gaze and replied, "You kicked a defenseless animal into the river!"

He brushed away that comment with a wave of his hand. "You've ruined this ceremony, to say nothing of your gown. Do you know how much I had to fork over to get this boat on such short notice? Now we'll have to reschedule—"

"I don't think so," Megan interrupted.

This statement, uncertain as it was, seemed to stun Winslow, who stared at her as though she was mad. "Meg, you don't mean that—"

"Yes, I do," she said, this time more forcefully. "And please, don't call me Meg."

He took a step toward her. "You're not thinking clearly."

"Yes, I am. Maybe for the first time in a long time—"

He covered her lips with one finger as if to silence her. "No, you're not. You don't want to spoil everything."

She batted at his hand. "I don't want to marry you," she stated flatly. "I don't think I *could* marry a man who did what you did and then gloated about it."

Mrs. Colpepper looked near to fainting. "Now, now, dear, wedding jitters, that's all." Turning her attention to John, she snapped, "How could you rescue the cat before you came to the aid of Robert Winslow?"

"Easy," he said, looking for a way out of this mess. Besides marrying people, the other thing John Vermont wasn't all that crazy about was scenes. Emotional outbursts, accusations, yelling—all this drove him nuts. He tried getting his cat away from Megan, thinking to himself that he could herd everyone up the ladder, deposit the cat in his cabin and get the *Ruby Rose* back to the wharf in time for a stiff drink and a thick steak. But she wasn't letting go. Foggy Dew had all but disappeared in the increasingly ruined dress and Megan was too busy being mad to think of anything else.

"Is that what this is all about?" Winslow chided as though Megan had informed him there was a speck of lint on his lapel. "For heaven's sake, it's just a cat."

His tone of voice was so condescending that even if John hadn't already detested him, he would have been moved to react. "Where in the hell do you think you get off kicking a pregnant animal!" he yelled.

This was the voice that shook shellfish loose from their moorings, and for a second, it served to quell all the chatter. But the moment passed.

Mrs. Colpepper recovered first. "Captain Vermont! Really!"

Another voice piped in. "Mr. Winslow? Should I still be taping all of this?"

At that, everyone turned to see who had spoken. It was the gangly young man who was videotaping the ceremony.

He was currently standing on a chair to get a better view. The camcorder pressed to his face and the steady red light said he was still trying to do his job.

Winslow spat out the words. "Turn the damn thing off, you imbecile!"

"Don't talk to him like that!" Megan said.

Once again Winslow searched Megan's face with incredulous eyes. "Why in blazes do you give a hoot *how* I talk to *him?*"

"He's a human being—"

Winslow shook his head at an observation he apparently found inconsequential, then turned back to John. "Believe you me, you sorry excuse for a captain. When the owner of this company finds out how you allowed a...a...cat to destroy a thirty-thousand-dollar wedding, you'll be lucky to get a job swabbing decks!"

"Is that all that matters to you?" Megan demanded before John could jump in with the information that he was the owner of this company. "It's money, isn't it?" she added as though a light bulb had just blinked on in her brain. "Just money."

"So, you *are* mad about the prenuptial agreement," Winslow said with a know-it-all sneer. "I knew it!"

"What I am is mad at *you!*" she said vehemently. "All you think about is your money—"

"That didn't seem to be a problem for you when I was writing you and your uncle all those hefty checks," Winslow snapped.

"What! How dare you—"

He interrupted her with a laugh. "Grow up, Meg. Money is money. I have it, you don't, and we both know you aren't about to really break it off with me over a flea-bitten cat, so go fix yourself up—"

Her eyes clearly reflected her turbulent emotions as a smile slowly curved her lips. However, this smile, John suddenly realized, bore no resemblance to the earlier one that had so transformed her face. This smile lasted only a second. John had a feeling about what was going to happen next, but before he could react, Megan had interrupted her former fiancé's diatribe by reaching forward and, once again, shoving him off the boat.

A half dozen people sprang into action, either screaming or throwing enough life rings to save the doomed passengers of the *Titanic*. As John went to the rescue he saw Megan run up the stairs, one arm still holding Foggy Dew, the other clutching her skirt high so she could move easier. She disappeared from sight about the same time he yanked Robert Winslow out of the river. Again.

Megan ran with blind panic, knowing only that she had to get away from everyone, especially Robert. At the top of the stairs she found dozens of her wedding guests staring at her, unclear about what had happened. Those who knew her, like her friends, her mother and Uncle Adrian, started toward her, but Megan knew how they felt, knew what their reaction to her mutiny would be, and so she gathered the wet cat closer to her body and headed up the next flight of stairs.

She emerged on a landing next to a short passageway and ran toward the front of the ship. It ended at a door with a sign that read Bridge—Authorized Personnel Only. She didn't want the bridge, she didn't want people. There were two other doors, one on either side. Without pausing, she turned the knob of the door on the right, gasping with relief when it popped open. She threw herself into a heavily shadowed room, slamming the wooden door behind her, searching for and finding the lock, which she clicked with a trembling hand.

As though sensing where she was, the cat suddenly renewed her efforts to get free. Megan released her grip, but it took a few seconds to unhook all the claws from the lace. Tearing was inevitable, but at last the animal sprang down onto a thick, red Oriental carpet that partially covered a plank floor. Still wet and obviously pregnant, the pathetic little animal wobbled toward the single shaft of sunlight that made its way through a gap in the curtains.

Megan followed and, flinging the heavy drapes aside, flooded the room with light and warmth. Dispassionately, she took in the rich, wooden walls, the framed pictures of sturdy tugboats, the navy fabric and gold-braided trim, the brass fixtures, the long mirror on the back of a door, the small round table and four captain's chairs, the jacket draped casually across the back of one of the chairs.

The jacket brought immediate thoughts of Captain Vermont. She'd expected a jolly kind of man with twinkling eyes and silver hair to run a stern-wheeler, not the young, handsome, commanding figure who had appeared at the altar. In his early thirties, he wore a deep blue uniform, the long jacket emphasizing his height. No brass buttons or nautical cap, just longish black hair that blew in the breeze. Straight black eyebrows and piercing blue eyes seemed to brook no nonsense, nor did the expression he wore, one of slight disinterest and curious detachment, and yet he'd seemed genuinely concerned about the little gray cat.

And his voice. Rich and deep like a cup of exceptional coffee, a voice that gave tender words an edge and angry words an attitude impossible to ignore. She recalled how she'd latched on to his gaze as she'd stood at the altar, how suddenly her whirlwind courtship and hasty wedding had seemed all wrong. It was odd, but reflecting upon it now, she realized she'd gathered from the captain's steady gaze the strength she'd needed to overcome her panic and complete her vows.

A lot of good it had done. If a man who kicked an animal wasn't bad enough, she'd been on the verge of marrying a man who kicked an animal and then had the audacity to be proud of himself!

This after the scene that very morning when he'd informed her she would have to sign a prenuptial agreement before the ceremony or he wasn't going through with it. Maybe she was naive, but she'd thought marriage was supposed to be based on trust, faith and love. Had she been wrong on all three counts? She'd thought him a generous man who supported her career as fund-raiser for the Riverside Hospital. In that position, she was supposed to be discerning when it came to assessing people—ha!

Still, in the end, buckling under pressure, she'd signed on the dotted line. What else was she supposed to do with her mother and all those people waiting to watch her commit herself to a man for eternity? She suddenly realized that that was what marriage was supposed to be, a uniting of the heart and spirit for eternity. She felt dizzy.

This was what happened when you let stardust fall into your eyes. This was what happened when you believed in the fairy tale that men were strong and wise and protective, when you didn't rely on yourself, when you didn't use your head, when you let your mother's dreams and goals get confused with your own.

It seemed the price of a clearer vision of him was a sharper image of herself.

The cat had commenced what promised to be a long bath. Sunlight fell on Megan's face as she stood in front of the windows and closed her eyes. Soon, she knew, her hideaway would be discovered; her mother and Robert would begin a campaign to gain admittance to this cabin and she would have choices to make.

Well, let them come, she thought with renewed determination. Let them all come and see what good it will do!

Chapter Two

The stern-wheeler was alive with rampant rumors that ran the gamut from the truth to out-and-out fabrications. John's favorite was that Winslow had jumped overboard in a gallant effort to save the poor little cat that Megan had drop-kicked into the water because it had torn her wedding dress.

John gave orders for the ship to weigh anchor and head back toward the dock in Portland. He told Winslow's family that since everything was paid for—one way or another—folks might as well eat and the band might as well play. Winslow promised a lawsuit, which brought a glint to John's eye and a challenging grin to his lips.

And then Megan's family came forward, all two of them. One was a rotund man of fifty and the other a middle-aged woman who must have once been a knockout. She nailed John with pale blue eyes and gripped his arm. She told him she'd heard that Megan had dunked poor Robert. It wasn't true, was it?

He assured her it was.

"Is my daughter nuts?" the woman asked. "The man is loaded."

John didn't answer her. Instead he said, "You're the bride's mother?"

The woman nodded. "We didn't meet last night at the rehearsal. Your event coordinator, Mrs. Colpepper, said you were busy..." Her voice trailed off as she waited for him to fill in the gap.

What he'd been busy doing was painting the kitchen at the house he was building high above the river. Mrs. Colpepper had read him the riot act for not showing up for the rehearsal, but jeez, he hated those things. If anything, they were worse than the actual ceremony. Marrying people was bad enough—practicing marrying people just seemed like cruel and unusual punishment.

Besides, it was a simple ceremony aboard a moored boat—what did they need to rehearse that for? As soon as he found a replacement for Colpepper, rehearsals were going to be the first thing to go. For now, he addressed the mother, "So, where is your daughter?"

The older woman gestured at the stairs. "Up there. She didn't want to talk to me or any of her friends, or even her uncle Adrian. She didn't even slow down when she saw us. I tell you, if her father, rest his soul, was here, *he* would have made her stop and listen to reason." She turned to the man beside her and added, "My George was *just* like Robert, wasn't he, Adrian?"

"In many ways, Lori," a big florid man with a fleshy nose and a small mouth said. "Don't worry, by now the girl's probably rigid with regret." The man stuck out a meaty hand and added, "Name's Adrian Haskell, Megan's uncle. I know how crazy the girl is about the Winslow chap. I'm sure we'll get this fracas cleared up."

"Where *is* poor Robert?" Megan's mother asked.

"Down below," John answered curtly. He was annoyed with Megan's family's reaction. He had to make a point of reminding himself that he didn't care about this melo-drama and if these misdirected people wanted to worry about the wrong party in this mess, then that was *their* business, not his.

He was almost at the top of the stairs when he heard his name yelled. He turned, knowing before he saw her that Mrs. Colpepper was about to tear into him again.

She stood at the bottom of the stairs, a plump woman swathed in lilac, prone to fussiness, enamored of protocol except when it came to her dealings with him.

"Listen here, Captain Vermont," she said through grit-ted teeth. "I hold you fully responsible for this fiasco. If you had forbidden that cat from coming aboard as I asked you to, none of this would have happened. And then to save it before you attended to Mr. Winslow was absolutely unpardonable. I have half a mind to tender my resignation. Why, when I think of the scandal—"

"Keep everyone else down there until I find out what the blazes is going on, Colpepper, you got that?" he in-terrupted.

"I have no intention of denying Mr. Winslow access to his bride—"

"*Especially* Mr. Winslow."

"But—"

He cut her off by turning his back and resuming the climb, Mrs. Colpepper's continuing diatribe as monoto-nous as the thumping slap of the boat's stern paddle.

Besides the wheelhouse, there were two cabins on the top deck, including his own. The cabin on the left opened to reveal a dark room, the event consultant's shipside of-fice. As he flipped on the light, he called Megan's name. Empty.

The other cabin—his cabin—was locked. Since he hadn't locked it, Megan must be holed up inside. He patted his pocket for the key, realizing at last that it was in his other jacket...which was behind the door with the distraught bride. This left him no alternative but to knock.

"Who is it?" she said at once as though she'd been standing on the other side of the door, waiting.

"It's Captain Vermont," he said sternly, not at all amused she'd chosen his private quarters in which to take sanctuary.

"Please, just go away," she said.

"Can't do that," he told her.

"Why not?"

"Open the door and we'll talk."

"No."

"There are over a hundred people out here wanting to see you," he told her.

"Well, I don't want to see them," she replied immediately.

"Just talk to me, then," he said.

A long pause was followed by, "Are you alone?"

He looked down the empty passageway. "For the moment."

"Can't you just steer the boat back to Portland and leave me be?" she pleaded.

"Maybe I can, but I'm not going to," he informed her.

Another long pause, then the door opened. Megan made no movement to step aside so John could enter.

"May I come in?"

"What do you want?"

He tapped the brass plaque attached to the mahogany door and said, "This is my cabin."

Biting her lip, she said, "I'm sorry. I really am."

John looked under her arm and saw Foggy Dew stretched out in the sunshine, licking an extended leg, her bulging middle attesting to the fact that she'd managed to hold on to the kittens. "Is the cat—"

"She's fine. She's almost dry."

"But you're scratched," he said, nodding at her right

arm. He didn't mention what she looked like—how the tears had reddened her eyes, how the designer dress was now tattered and torn, stained with blood, cat hair and river water, how the flowers in her hair had slipped down to just above her left ear. Heck, none of these things detracted from the winsome beauty that was her birthright. Again, he noticed her high cheekbones and the flawless texture of her skin, the wispy blond strands that curled around her hairline, the cupid's bow shape of her lips, lips absolutely begging to be kissed. John felt a deep jolt. Where in the world were these kind of thoughts coming from?

She stared down at her arm as though aware for the first time that rescuing Foggy Dew had extracted a toll.

He cleared his throat. "Come across the hall and I'll find the first-aid kit. I know Mrs. Colpepper keeps it in her office. We'll get you fixed up."

"It's not necessary, it doesn't matter."

He tried a different angle to budge her. "I know your mother and your fiancé want to see you. You go to Mrs. Colpepper's office and I'll escort them—"

"I don't ever want to see Robert Winslow again," she stated firmly. "He's a jerk."

Was it really possible this was the first time she'd noticed what a creep the guy was? Remembering he was not a counselor but a captain, he mumbled, "I, uh, happen to know there's a certain amount of…of strain associated with getting married…"

She was shaking her head and new tears were puddling in her eyes. "I thought I could talk to them. I know I'm being evasive, but I need time to think. I just can't face them all right now—you tell them for me, okay?"

"Miss Morison—"

"Please," she added, and with an apologetic shrug, slowly closed the door again, leaving John Vermont high and dry and out of a cabin.

He pounded a fist against his leg as he strode down the

passageway, determined to find a new captain for this ship pronto. "Damn weddings," he swore beneath his breath.

An hour later he gave up trying to restrain Megan's fiancé, figuring that by now she'd probably had second thoughts and was ready to come out and talk...and give him back his cabin.

"Meg? Listen to me. Open the door and let me in." Winslow's voice was cajoling.

John stood across the passageway, leaning against a bulkhead, arms crossed, watching.

"No," she said.

John shook his head. He was beginning to suspect that nothing short of dynamite was going to blast that woman from his cabin, certainly not this bozo's entreaties. Despite his fervent wish she'd leave, he had to admit a certain amount of admiration for her tenacity.

"I will not go away," Winslow said. He'd stripped off the tuxedo jacket but still wore the black slacks, the white shirt and the suspenders, all of which had dried, to a point, as had his hair, but his shoes squeaked when he moved. While his voice was still persuasive, his appearance had taken a definite nosedive. He didn't look quite so smug now.

Running a hand through his damp hair and lowering his voice, Winslow talked to the door. "You're acting like a child," he said, his voice as smooth as an oil slick. "You know that, don't you, Meg? Like a little child, running away, scared and silly. Your behavior is embarrassing me and your family. Heck, it was just a stupid animal, and besides, the big brave captain rescued it, so what's the harm? Now, come out here. Open the door."

At his side, John's hand rolled into a fist, almost ready to give Winslow the thump on the head he'd been asking for. He was unclear whether his desire to beat the tar out of this guy had to do with the degrading way he addressed

Megan, his total disregard for animals, or the jab at himself. But the door stayed shut and retreating footsteps behind it announced clearly that Megan had moved back into the room, ending this conversation.

Winslow turned, his sour expression growing even more surly when he found John staring at him. "I hear you own this tub," he growled.

John nodded.

"Then redeem yourself a little and open the door. You must have a key."

John smiled. "Actually, I don't."

"Then break the lock—"

"And do what, Mr. Winslow? Drag the lady out by her hair? Dump her in the river like she dumped you? Make her walk the plank, keelhaul her, put her in shackles and lock her in the brig?"

For once the man seemed at a loss for words. He moved a few steps away, then turned back and glared at John. "I'm not through with you yet, Vermont! I have friends in high places."

"Good for you," John said as he pushed himself away from the wall and opened the door to the bridge, anxious only to return *Ruby Rose* to shore and get these people off his boat.

Megan closed the drapes and flicked on a lamp. For the first time she caught sight of herself in the long mirror, and she winced. Without pausing to think, she stripped off her wedding dress and tore the ridiculous flowers from her hair, dumping both on the floor.

Little doubts started to kick in as she found a bathroom behind the door with the mirror and washed the blood off her arm. Had she overreacted? Had she, like Robert said, been silly? Did the captain think she was silly? She suddenly had the intense desire to know what he thought, but since there was no way of finding him without risking running into her family and Robert, she decided to stay put.

Four angry red lines attested to the cat's plight and helped ease Megan's doubts. She rubbed soap into the wounds, rinsed them carefully, then splashed her face with cold water, pausing to look out the porthole beside the sink. The shoreline was turning from rural to city, which meant they must be close to the wharf.

Back in the cabin she was faced with the prospect of waiting to disembark in her underwear or donning the captain's spare jacket. As she took it off the back of the chair, she wondered how, and if, she would have the nerve to face everyone. She buttoned all the black buttons. Seeing as she was just a touch over five-five, a good ten inches shorter than Captain Vermont, the jacket fell to below her knees and swamped her. She rolled up the cuffs. It was better than the dress. Anything was better than the dress.

Besides, the garment's lining slipped easily against her bare skin while the collar was rough against her neck. It smelled of musk, as though aftershave had left its trail. It was like being wrapped in an embrace, comforting somehow. She turned up the collar and hugged the jacket close to her body.

She watched the docking process from the safety of the captain's cabin, ignoring the repeated pleas that came from the passageway, pleas that begged her to come to her senses.

"I already have," she whispered.

There was always a feeling of satisfaction when a voyage, no matter how small, was successfully completed, but this time the final docking of the *Ruby Rose* at the old wharf along the waterfront brought its captain a particularly gratifying wave of relief.

As John took off his gloves and opened the shallow drawer in which he kept them, he suffered the good-natured ribbing of his first mate, Danny Borel. Danny, aware of the wedding fracas, found it especially funny that John was out of a cabin.

As Danny left the bridge for a hot date with a leggy redhead he'd met on deck, John's eyes fell on the extra set of keys in the drawer. Snapping them up, he tossed them into the air and caught them, chuckling to himself. *Now we'll see…*

The first order of business was a post-voyage stroll around each of the three decks. Though he tried to avoid her, Colpepper was lurking by the stairs, waiting for him.

"I have half a mind to quit," she sputtered.

He thought she had half a mind—period. He said, "It's been a long day, Colpepper."

"When I think of the hours I spent—"

Holding up his hand and darting down the stairs, he called, "Save it for tomorrow, will you?"

He snatched an extra bottle of champagne and a couple of spare lobsters off the ravaged buffet table and, thus armed, went back to his cabin and knocked on the door.

He heard music from within, but no one answered the knock. A muffled meow prompted him to use the spare key.

Foggy Dew sat in the middle of the small room, blinking her yellow eyes. John nudged the door closed with his elbow, set the tray on the round table, and picked the cat up, stroking her head.

"You caused a heap of trouble today," he told the cat right before he spotted the mound of lacy white material in the corner, and in the next glance, Megan, asleep on his bunk, dressed in one of his jackets, her long bare legs crossed at the ankles, her hands resting on her flat stomach. The cat struggled to get down. John set her carefully on the rug, somewhat surprised to see her jump up on the bunk and curl into a ball by Megan's hip.

For some time he stood off to the side, watching the

peaceful—and tantalizing—rise and fall of Megan's chest as she breathed, admiring the thick sweep of lashes that lay against her cheeks, the gentle repose of her mouth. And, once again, he imagined covering her succulent lips with his own. He imagined gathering her in his arms and kissing her awake. He imagined the look in her eyes....

He shook his head. Crazy thoughts! Ridiculous, inappropriate thoughts he had no business thinking. He made himself turn away from her and all the nebulous yearnings she seemed to inspire.

The sideboard produced silverware, napkins, water glasses. He opened the wine, poured himself a couple of inches and sat in one of the chairs, propping his feet up on another. Megan Morison was as easy on the eyes as she was stubborn, all right. He wanted her to wake up but he suspected when she did she'd start fussing, so he let her be.

The evening was wearing away when she finally stirred. She awoke slowly, and John watched, knowing all the while she was unaware of his presence, knowing he should announce himself. But he liked seeing her yawn and stretch, liked the way her lips curved when she saw the cat beside her. When she finally turned her head and saw him gazing at her, she sat up abruptly, tugging modestly on the jacket.

He poured her a hefty glass of champagne. "Are you thirsty?"

Getting to her feet, she said, "I haven't eaten or slept in four days, so I guess what I am is hungry."

He gestured at the lobsters but she didn't seem to notice.

"I borrowed your jacket," she told him as she brushed her hands down the front.

"It looks good on you."

"I just had to change. I hope you don't mind—"

"Not at all, Miss Morison. Fact is, I think it looks better on you than that fancy dress..."

He stopped talking because her eyes had suddenly filled with tears. Obviously he'd said the wrong thing.

"I—I'm sorry," he said as he pushed the plate forward. "Here, I brought lobster, have some."

"I hate lobster," she said as she wiped tears off her cheeks with the cuff of her—his—jacket.

"But it's from your wedding…well, almost wedding…"

His voice trailed off because what he'd said had brought forth more waterworks. He handed her a napkin, which she used to mop at her face, and then she sat opposite him.

"It was Robert's idea to have it. I wanted chicken. Where is everybody?"

"They're gone."

"All of them?"

"I dropped them off at the loading pier before bringing the boat down here to her permanent berth. I'm afraid I took it upon myself to persuade your family to leave you alone. I guess you want to hear that your fiancé was very hard to convince—"

"No," she interrupted.

John shrugged. "Your mother said to remind you that you don't have an apartment anymore so to come to her house. I promised her you'd get home okay."

More tears as Megan stared at the hated crustaceans. When she'd recovered from the new onslaught, she added, "I forgot…I gave up my place so that after the honeymoon I could…I could move in with…with…Robert."

"Well, maybe you two will patch things up."

She shook her head in a desultory fashion.

John fished a piece of lobster out of the shell and held it low to the ground. Foggy Dew stared at it for a second, apparently decided it was worth the effort of moving, and jumped down from the bunk. He set the morsel on the floor and turned his attention back to Megan, wondering how he could politely ask her to leave. The half-naked beauty was intended for another man, but she was starting to make him want things he had no business wanting.

He said, "Well, it's getting late—"

She glanced at the clock that hung on a bulkhead next to the barometer, but said nothing.

"I sent a crew member down to the bridal dressing room and she retrieved the clothing you arrived in. It's across the hall." To himself he added that it was a damn shame she had to get out of his jacket. He liked the way the navy blue looked next to her cap of yellow hair, the way different parts of her anatomy filled out the cloth in ways the tailor hadn't intended.

"That was very kind of you," she said.

Looking into her eyes was like glimpsing two blue gems buried in the depths of a mountain spring. He had to make himself turn away and liberate more lobster for the cat. "I can call you a cab—"

"I have nowhere to go," she said.

John delivered the lobster, took a long swallow of champagne and eyed her above the rim of the glass. Then he said, "But your mother—"

"You don't understand," she said as she pushed herself away from the table and began pacing. "My mother is crazy about Robert Winslow. She thinks the sun rises and sets on his bank account. All she ever talks about is how much he's like my late father."

"Is he?" John heard himself ask.

She shrugged. "Yes. Oh, I don't know. Dad was strong-willed and blustery, but he was also kind. I can't even imagine him attacking a harmless animal like that. Anyway, he died when I was just a little kid." She blinked away the past and added, "Mom will spend the entire night trying to get me to see the stupidity of my ways. I can't face her."

John's gaze had dropped to her smooth, shapely legs. Looking up, he said, "Then that uncle of yours—"

"If anything, he loves Robert even more than Mom does. Robert has given Uncle Adrian money for bailing out a sick business. My uncle's first thought is going to be that I'm jeopardizing the business by jilting Robert. I can't go to him, I just can't."

"Friends?"

"Don't you see? *Everyone* likes Robert Winslow. He throws money around like there's no tomorrow. He buys people's affections."

John surprised himself by asking, "Did he buy yours, too?"

She stopped pacing and stared at him. More tears filled her eyes as she said, "No, of course not." But she ruined the validity of her denial by immediately adding, "At least I don't think he did."

Right... John thought. She kind of reminded him of Betsy, his first love, his ex-wife, who had married him on a whim, intrigued by his wealth. Within six months she'd grown bored with his work ethic and taken up extracurricular activities of her own. It had cost him a hefty one-time payment to rid his life of Betsy, and though she'd cheated and lied to him, he'd still felt like the world had been torn asunder when she closed the door behind her. That had been two years ago, and it was only within the past eight or nine months that he'd begun to see that *her* leaving was really *him* escaping. Who needed women? They were fickle and hard on the old heart—a man was better off without them.

"I wish you'd say something," Megan said uneasily.

"I don't know what to say," he told her.

Grasping the back of a chair with both hands and leaning slightly forward, she fixed him with an intent stare. "Do you think I was silly today? Do you think I acted irrationally?"

He grinned. "Let's just say that if you hadn't pushed that idiot off my boat, I would have."

"Thanks."

"No problem."

"Wait, did you say this was *your* boat? Does that mean you won't lose your job because of me?" The relief in her voice touched John. She'd been worried about his fate in this mess—that was kind of sweet.

He laughed and said, "No such luck. Now, like I said, it's getting late—"

"I don't have a job," she said suddenly, as though just realizing that even that part of her life was screwed up.

"You quit your job?"

Though her voice grew husky and her chin trembled, she held her head high, apparently straining for control. "I quit it as of two weeks ago. After all, I was marrying Robert Winslow, what did I need to work at a hospital for? I was going to work with him—at least, that was my plan. I found out this morning that that wasn't *his* plan, however. He didn't want me anywhere near his business or his precious money."

John remained silent. He suspected her shattered life had derailed her tongue.

"I don't know where to go or what to do," she said softly.

John rubbed his jaw as he thought. Heck, where she went wasn't his problem, was it? He was a skipper of a stern-wheeler, not director of a lonely heart's club. What did she expect of him? He said, "Maybe a hotel?"

A brief look of hope was extinguished by a frown that tugged on the corners of her lips. Sighing heavily, she shook her head. "I might as well go to Mom's house. I'll have to face her sooner or later. Maybe she'll take pity and let me be for one night."

"I'm sure that's the logical thing to do," he told her, relieved she'd come to her senses. He'd been afraid of what might have happened if she'd insisted on staying the night.

"Is there a phone on board so I can call a cab?"

"Better than that," he said, generosity filling his heart. "I'll give you a lift on my way home."

She looked startled. Gesturing at the table and the sideboard, the bed and the console that held a stereo and TV-VCR combination, she said, "Don't you live here, in this room, on this boat?"

Standing, he looked down at her. "Sometimes I spend the night, but not often. I'm building a little house along the river, an hour or so from here, and that's where I live. For now, until I find someone else to skipper this boat, I'm commuting back and forth every day."

"Even on a Sunday?"

"Especially on a Sunday."

The mention of work reminded him that Mrs. Colpepper had abandoned ship, supposedly for good. As much as she drove him crazy, he wasn't prepared to lose her just weeks before a big media dinner-dance she'd booked.

Well, she'd made threats before and she'd always come back—whether it was because of her generous salary, dedication to her obligations or just plain love of driving him nuts, John didn't know and didn't much care.

"Your offer is very generous," Megan murmured. "Thank you."

"No problem. I know this day hasn't exactly gone the way you'd planned..."

His voice petered out as Megan's eyes grew soft with tears she seemed determined to curtail. He'd said the wrong thing again. Mumbling something about fetching her clothes, John got to his feet and crossed the cabin, enjoying the shot of cool river air that hit his face when he opened the door.

You should have just called her a cab, you blasted fool, he grumbled to himself.

Foggy Dew had followed him outside. She made an odd noise as she rubbed his ankles. To John, it sounded as though she was agreeing.

Chapter Three

"Over there," Megan said, pointing to a hamburger stand visible through the rain as a blur of rainbow-colored lights. It had started drizzling as they'd left the stern-wheeler and had picked up gusto as they'd driven through town. Now it fell in relentless buckets. Megan imagined Captain Vermont was anxious to take her home and be rid of her, but there was no way she was going to face her mother on an empty stomach.

He stopped his truck in front of a smiling clown face and opened the window the old-fashioned way, with a handle. For an instant Megan flashed back to the steel cocoon of a cloud gray BMW, Robert beside her, lowering his window with a touch of a finger. This act never happened at a fast-food restaurant, banish the thought. Robert Winslow wouldn't be caught dead at anything as "ordinary" as a fast-food place—which made the act of stopping at this one all the more appealing!

"What do you want?" the captain asked as rain came through the open window, pelting his shoulder with glistening drops.

Ah, to be asked. Robert had deplored her bad eating habits, endlessly pointing out what was good for her and what wasn't, taking it upon himself to wean her from junk food. A fitness freak, he jogged and biked—in fact, the only sport he didn't train in was swimming, a thought that brought an evil little smile to Megan's lips. "I'll have a hamburger. No, wait, make it a cheeseburger. And French fries. And a milk shake."

Without comment on her choices, the captain repeated her order into the clown's mouth and a disembodied voice told them to drive forward.

"Don't you want anything?" she asked as she fished the last twenty-dollar bill from the depths of her wallet. "My treat."

"Thanks, anyway, but I'm not hungry," he said as he took the money and advanced to the drive-in window. She watched as he paid the attendant, handed Megan back the change and then accepted the food. He had a strong profile visible because of the restaurant lights. A good nose, chiseled jawline, interesting mouth. He was a big man, but not the least bit bulky. A man who exuded confidence and yet seemed strangely ill-at-ease when he was around her.

How could she blame him? She'd been hesitant and scared during the ceremony, mad as a hornet when Robert kicked that poor little kitty into the river, and an emotional wreck ever since. No wonder he was skittish!

He drove as the windshield wipers whacked back and forth and the rain increased. There was nothing like Oregon rain, she thought. She pushed aside the next thought, that if she hadn't shoved Robert overboard, she'd now be on her way to Australia, where it was probably warm and dry. Wait, that wasn't right. If Robert hadn't kicked the little cat, they'd *both* be on their way to Australia.

And if that had happened, if the wedding had gone as planned, would she now be delirious with joy or facing the possibility she'd made the biggest mistake of her life? If the wedding had gone as planned, they wouldn't have thrown accusations at each other; he wouldn't have accused her of marrying him for his money.

This thought made her insides boil with righteous indignation. She'd never taken a penny from him, not a penny! The checks he had written were for the hospital's new rehab center, for which she'd been raising funds when she'd met him, and yet he'd made it sound as if they were personal handouts.

And since when was she responsible for Uncle Adrian's debts? If Robert hadn't wanted to bail him out, then he shouldn't have bailed him out!

The truth of the matter was that she'd used almost every dime in her savings and pushed her credit cards to their limits to buy her elaborate wedding dress, bowing to pressure from her mother to make sure it was a gown that wouldn't "embarrass" Robert. He'd insisted on a fancy wedding and had offered to pay for it, and as Megan didn't have the funds to finance it herself, nor did her mother, she'd agreed. In retrospect, she'd agreed to everything: rushing into marriage, a gala ceremony she couldn't afford, a dress that put her in debt, a prenuptial agreement that should have been the last straw.

She'd been caught in a whirlwind of romance, so enamored by the fact that an important man like Winslow would make such obvious ploys to win her, and so pleased to have her mother happy again, that she'd put her brain on hold. *Well, I won't let it happen again,* she swore to herself. *I'll get my life back on track. I'm independent, I don't need a man to define myself. It's foolish and it's dangerous. For me, romance is dead!*

"What did you say?"

The sound of the captain's deep voice startled her, sending a few French fries tumbling to her lap. She hadn't realized she'd spoken out loud. How much had she mumbled? How much had he heard?

"Nothing," she muttered as she retrieved errant fries.

"You're not eating much."

"I guess I wasn't as hungry as I thought," she told him as she dumped the leftovers into the sack. It was depressing to realize Robert's eating habits had become hers, as well.

She pointed toward the windshield and added, "We're almost there, take the next left."

Megan's mother lived on the same heavily wooded street on which Megan had grown up. Back then, the house had been luxurious and comfortable, a meeting place for her father's many friends, a warm house full of laughter. Times had changed; the house was now in need of extensive repairs, the neighborhood was turning seedy, and her mother was holding on by a string. Megan had hoped to help her mom relocate after her honeymoon—that dream was gone now, too.

It had been a very wet, windy winter and a few of the trees had fallen, leaving gaps in the familiar landscape. One fallen tree lay across the front of a neighboring yard, waiting to be hacked into firewood, the root ball positioned toward the road. In the dark and through the rain, the giant fistlike roots clutched the earth in a last, futile attempt to ward off the inevitable.

The house was a two-story white Colonial, lit to within an inch of its life. It never failed to amaze Megan how much better the place looked at night than in the unforgiving glare of day, when the missing shutters, peeling paint, sagging eaves and cracked brick drew attention to themselves. In the driveway sat a sleek gray car, which sent Megan's heart into overload.

"Don't stop!" she squealed as Captain Vermont slowed and approached the curb.

He flashed her an annoyed frown. "But that's the place. Your mother said it was white and—"

"I grew up here. You think I don't know my own house? Don't you see? It's Robert's car. He must be here. Keep going."

"But, Megan, Miss Morison—"

"Just keep going!" she demanded as she saw Robert step in front of the living room window, glass in hand.

Her mother was entertaining him! Knowing how Megan felt, her mother had nevertheless invited Robert Winslow into the house and given him a cold drink—no doubt cranberry juice and gin. What a traitor! Her own mother cavorting with the enemy! How dare she!

"Turn down here," she told the captain.

He shot her a quick look before following her directions, traveling another half a block along a dark, empty side street before pulling up to the curb. Sighing heavily, he turned to face her. "Now what?" he asked, his voice a lot drier than the weather.

Megan wanted him to keep moving. Her heart was beating so fast it pounded in her ears and she had the irrational notion that somehow Robert had known that the green vehicle rolling past the house belonged to Captain Vermont and that she was inside. She fought the desire to turn around to make sure he wasn't running down the street after them.

"Now what?" he repeated.

Megan glanced over her shoulder. The side street was empty save a few million raindrops that splattered on the pavement and ran in torrents down the gutters.

"I can't believe my mother is visiting with that man." She was practically fuming.

"Obviously they're waiting for you to come home."

She took a steadying breath.

"Are you ready now?" he asked her.

"Ready? Ready for what?"

"To go back to your mom's house—"

"Heaven's no!" she screeched. Oh, how she yearned for her lost apartment, for the solitude she craved, for time to curl into a ball and sleep, sleep, sleep. With that option lost, the next best thing would be a motel, but she knew her credit card would tilt any machine it was run through. Unless the department store she still had credit at had suddenly gone into the business of renting beds or she could find a place that charged less than fifteen dollars, she was out of luck.

She lowered her voice. "Would you mind taking me to Uncle Adrian's house? It's not far."

The captain's silence filled the truck as surely as a ton of mud. Rarely in Megan's twenty-six years had she felt as isolated as she did at that moment. This man's silent condemnation of her character cut her to the quick. With the speed and warning of a flash flood, her emotions overcame her, enveloped her, coaching yet more tears from her eyes and a hopeless sob from her throat.

Temporarily oblivious to anything but her own pain and frustration, Megan was startled when she felt two strong hands grip her shoulders. She looked up to see that the captain had moved close to her. Slowly, cautiously, he pulled her toward him, folding his arms around her. She was so miserable she lay her head against his hard chest, the edge of a black button biting into her cheek. He slowly patted her on the back, she assumed to offer comfort, and oddly enough, his embrace did just that—it comforted her.

There was a feeling of safety to be held so gingerly, so carefully. He smelled like fresh air, and the warmth of his exhaled breaths touched her bare neck. It was with a sense of alarm that she suddenly noticed she was enjoying his attention. She straightened immediately. She would not leap from one man's arms into another's, even if the current pair were strong and welcoming in their hesitant, gentle way, and even if these arms were offering nothing but solace.

He released her immediately, but she could feel his eyes on her. She felt set adrift, anchorless and thoroughly alarmed. "Thank you," she whispered.

He gave her a napkin that had escaped the fast-food restaurant cleanup.

"I don't even know your name. Your first name, I mean."

"Jonathan," he said. "John."

"John," she repeated.

"Are you feeling better now?"

She nodded. "I'm really not like this, weepy and everything. Normally, I'm very controlled."

"I'm sure you are," he said, his wonderful voice sounding anything but sure.

"I'm sorry I'm such a pain—"

"I'm the one who's sorry," he said, cutting her off. "I was rude. I'd chalk it up to stress or fatigue, but I believe you've cornered the markets in those departments. No, please don't cry again, Megan. Okay, where does your uncle live?"

She willed the tears she could feel burning behind her eyes to stay put. "Three miles east of here, even further out of town. I know it's late—"

"I live another ten miles east of that, so you can see it's no bother. Besides, in few minutes you'll be with your uncle. Family, that's what you need at a time like this. The welcoming embrace of your family. Just tell me when to turn."

He hadn't said it but what Megan knew he meant was three more miles and he'd get this crazy woman out of his car and out of his life!

The drive was made in silence. As Megan was reluctant to get back on the main street, she guided him through the back roads, which made the drive twice as long, but if he noticed the discrepancy, he didn't mention it.

Until recently Uncle Adrian had lived in a condominium right in the heart of Portland. Business problems had forced him to downgrade his life-style, so that now his address was rural. In fact, it would be almost impossible to imagine any place further removed from his former abode than his present dwelling, a little tract house so close to the street there wasn't even room for a sidewalk.

Well, that wouldn't last, not now that good old Robert had bailed the business out of a hole. Soon, thanks to Robert, Uncle Adrian would be moving back to town. That was, *if* Robert didn't rescind his help and leave Uncle Adrian high and dry— Good grief, what in the world had made Megan think she'd be welcome here?

It was too late to change her mind, though, she decided after another peek at John's profile. He yawned into his hand and rubbed his temple, and she sat back, prepared to take on Uncle Adrian.

"It's the pink one," Megan said, gesturing to the humble little house right before she caught sight of the gray car pulling into the narrow driveway. Red taillights flicked off as she watched, and the driver's door opened. Robert dashed between the car and the house.

"Don't stop," she snapped. "Don't stop!"

"Not again?"

"I should have known. Robert isn't the kind of man to sit by the telephone while another person affects his fate, especially me. He'll keep checking everywhere he thinks I might go until he finds me."

The captain kept driving. "How did he get here before us?"

"I took all that time blubbering," she mumbled.

Half a mile down the road, John pulled the truck to the curb, turned off the ignition and once again stared at her.

"You can't avoid your family forever," he said softly,

his voice comforting now, warm and easy, all hint of sarcasm gone.

"I can try."

"Sooner or later, you're going to have to face them."

"Listen, John," she said boldly. "Sooner or later I will face them. Sooner or later, I'll tell them all to back off and leave me alone. I'll rebuild my life, hold my chin up high and be a role model for women everywhere. But why do I have to do it tonight? Why can't I have just one night to sort out my thoughts and get my life back in order? Is that so much to ask?"

"I suppose not," he admitted. With a flick, he turned on the interior lights. She saw him glance at his watch.

"What time is it?"

"Almost midnight."

"Oh, brother, no wonder I feel like a sack of cement. I'm so sorry—"

Smothering another yawn with his fist, he waved her apologies aside. "Megan, I'll be frank with you. I have to get up and drive back down to the pier at six o'clock tomorrow morning because there's a guy coming to service the navigation equipment, then I have to marry two couples, which is an ordeal for me even when I'm well rested. I live twenty minutes from here. I have a guest house. Why don't you come to my place, spend the night with the door firmly locked and all the privacy you could possibly want, and tomorrow I'll drive you anywhere you desire. How about it?"

No getting around it, his plan had appeal. For one thing, she didn't have the nerve to ask him to drive her back into town where she might bunk with a girlfriend. Besides, Robert would never dream to look for her at this man's house and she really did need a little time to get her head on straight. She snuck a peek at John Vermont and found his expression had changed from earnest to alarmed and she wondered what she'd done to warrant it. Too tired to worry about his feelings when her own were such a quagmire, she said, "Thanks. I'll take you up on your offer."

He nodded. He didn't look the least bit pleased. Megan added, "I'll call my mom from your house so she won't call out the national guard."

"The car phone is right in front of you. Help yourself," he said.

Megan picked up the phone and made the call. She was evasive about where she was and with whom and promised to call again tomorrow.

Tomorrow. How could a word that promised distance suddenly loom so prominently on the horizon?

Twenty minutes later John opened the door of his house and ushered Megan Morison inside. He was immediately set upon by his yellow Lab, Lily, who licked his hand, wagged her tail, cast Megan a wary look and shot into the night.

John saw Megan's gaze drift from the tile floors to the loft area above. When she lowered her eyes and looked into the main room, he knew she took in the wall of windows that faced the river, though it was so dark and wet now that the beauty outside was invisible.

"Obviously a man's place," she said as she looked around. "Is there a Mrs. Vermont?"

"There was. There isn't anymore."

"Oh…I'm sorry."

"Don't be. I'm even worse in the marriage department than you are."

This comment made her eyes glisten. John mentally kicked himself for once again inserting his foot into his mouth as he crossed the room and opened one of the large sliding-glass doors. Lily wandered in, beaded raindrops on her yellow coat. She spared Megan another speculative glance, then moseyed over to the woven rug that sat in front of the huge stone fireplace.

Why had he brought her here? From the moment the offer had left his lips, he'd known it was a mistake. It was just that for a second he'd been overcome by a protective streak he couldn't explain, one he didn't even like. Rescuing women was a fool's errand—he'd done it once with Betsy and he wasn't going to do it again. He glanced back at Megan and the memory of holding her swamped him, the soft, yielding quality of her body, the smell of her hair. She was so beautiful. Was that it?

"This room is huge," she said, taking a step toward him.

"I like my space," he said with a little too much emphasis on the second and last words.

She nodded curtly as though the message he had inadvertently delivered was received and noted. Then she smiled at him, bit her bottom lip and bowed her head, staring down at the floor. It was a cunning gesture that told him very clearly she was sensing his unease and found it amusing.

Egads, he realized with a start. It wasn't just her current vulnerability that attracted him. It wasn't just her big blue eyes or her body, either. Those things were distractions, sure, but distractions that were relatively easy to dismiss. After all, there were lots of pretty and needy women in the world.

What Megan possessed was far more dangerous. There was a light in her eyes, a directness about her he found compelling, a sense of play and wonder that surfaced even when she was distressed. And there was that tenacious streak he'd witnessed, too. If it wasn't such a cliché, he'd be damned tempted to say the woman had spunk!

She had moved toward the sofa and was standing beside Lily. The two eyed each other with mutual distrust. Megan said, "I don't think your dog likes me."

"She's never been overly fond of women."

"The jealous type, huh?"

He shrugged.

Megan hugged herself as though she was cold. "You really love your animals, don't you?"

He made himself stop looking at her, stop thinking about her. For a time after Betsy had left, he'd wondered if he'd ever want to get involved with a woman again and now he was discovering the answer was a resounding yes. But this one? She didn't seem a very good prospect. He vowed to stop thinking about her.

He glanced at his dog and said, "Lily is family. I used to own a dozen tugboats and she was like a mascot. I can't take her on the stern-wheeler because she has a bad habit of chasing cats and Foggy Dew has squatter's rights." He chanced another look at Megan and added, "Shall I start a fire? Do you want something to eat or drink?"

"Actually, I'm just exhausted."

"I'll show you to your room."

He was aware of her following him to the sliding-glass door. He flicked on the outside light, illuminating some of the stone patio. "There's an umbrella hanging on the hook to your left," he told her and waited while she opened it. She held it high enough to shield him from the rain, too, and together they quickly moved toward a small dark building to the right. A motion sensor caught their movement and showered them with light.

The guest house was no more than a bedroom and a bath, built first so John and Betsy would have someplace to sleep while he built the larger house. Betsy had left before the house was completed so she'd never stepped foot in it. But this little room always made him think of her and he seldom used it now. It was cold inside, and he switched on a lamp before finding the thermostat and turning up the heat.

"Come on in," he told Megan, who had folded the umbrella and propped it next to the door. She passed in front of him, brushing his chest with her shoulder. Glancing up at him, she muttered a quick, "Sorry." It seemed guileless enough, but the way his heart raced when she'd touched him made him feel as if he was standing on the edge of a swollen river, poised to tumble into the roiled depths.

"The bathroom is over there. Extra toothbrushes and things are in the top drawer. I'll get you another blanket."

She looked around the room, then stared right into his eyes. "You own that big stern-wheeler, and this house is spectacular. It must be worth a bundle."

He narrowed his eyes and nodded cautiously. "I suppose."

"Which means you have a lot of money."

Frowning, John replied, "I guess you could say that."

"Hmm…" she murmured as she turned toward the bed.

"I'll get the blanket," he told her, glad he'd made the decision not to think about her anymore. Hell, he'd judged her correctly right from the start. Winslow's words, spoken in anger, revisited John. *Money is money. I have it and you don't.*

It took him ten minutes to dash back to the house, track down a quilt and the nightshirt an aunt had sent him for Christmas and which he'd never used, and return. When he pushed the cracked door open, he found Megan sitting on the side of the bed, bleary-eyed, yawning. She rose, sparing him a weak smile.

"I brought you something to sleep in," he told her as he handed her the nightshirt. Odd, but he suddenly didn't feel the least big sleepy.

"Thank you, John. For everything, I mean."

He set the quilt down and backed out of the room. His mind was doing funny little things, like imagining her in the blue plaid flannel, her hair tousled, her feet bare, her eyes happy as they gazed into his…

"You're leaving?"

Was there a note of disappointment in her voice? He

stammered, "I know you have a lot of...of thinking to do—"

She interrupted him. "I'm way too tired to think. I'll think tomorrow. But I don't see an alarm clock and I don't want to keep you waiting in the morning."

John took a deep breath. For a second he'd thought she wanted him to stay and though he never in a million years would have—well, maybe never in a *hundred* years was more truthful—he still felt a slight disappointment to find her needs were centered on an alarm clock. "I'll knock on your door," he told her.

She yawned again, giving him his exit cue. Mumbling, "Good night," he closed and locked the door behind him, striding purposefully across the patio, welcoming the cool rain—nature's rendition of a cold shower—and putting distance between himself and Megan Morison. Tomorrow she'd be gone. Seeing as he couldn't seem to recall from one moment to the next that he was completely disinterested in her, this was a good thing. A very good thing.

Megan awoke slowly. Weak sunlight filtered into the room through open venetian blinds, and she realized with a start it was morning. Time to get up and face a day that promised to be almost as bad as the day before.

The heavy nightshirt reached all the way to her ankles, and she smiled to herself when she thought of the look on John's face when he'd handed it to her. He'd looked nervous. That was silly, but darned if it wasn't the way his expression struck her.

In the bathroom, while she stripped off the nightshirt and hooked it on the back of the door, she examined the pink marble floor and counter, the huge whirlpool bath with an enclosed garden visible through the adjoining window, the glass-encased shower, the skylights with the automated shades. The bathroom screamed money and something else—a feminine touch that the house lacked. How did she keep bumping into these wealthy types? Were they all like Robert, using their material gains to control their worlds?

The thought of Robert made her heart feel like an old, deflated tire. For weeks she'd imagined their futures linked. Now that they weren't, she needed to readjust her thinking, to go back to the way she was before Robert had appeared on the scene.

In a moment of honesty she admitted she'd at first been attracted by Robert's confidence, his control. A man like Robert seemed to command respect, or at least that's what she'd told herself. Maybe the truth of the matter was that he hadn't commanded it at all, he'd purchased it like one of his radio stations or that new villa in Rome he'd bragged about.

And then there'd been her mother, happy at last that Megan had found Mr. Wonderful.

Obviously, she'd been more than a little blind. As she waited for the water to heat, she stared at her forearm, at the angry red scratches put there by a terrified animal. Her next thought was of John, lifting the cat, giving it to her.

Two men, alike and yet different; one she'd thought she knew, one of whom she knew practically nothing.

The hot water helped take care of the melancholy. The top drawer yielded a toothbrush and a blue comb, which she used to style her hair. Without other options, she put back on the jeans and the red sweater, the loafers and the red socks with white hearts on the ankles, and opened the door.

A huge stone patio stretched before her, hugging the contours of the land. Megan was drawn toward the rock wall that surrounded it. She perched on the edge for a minute, looking down toward the river below. John had a dock attached to his land and attached to the dock was a small boat.

A glance at the sky revealed dense clouds overhead.

Obviously it was going to rain today, and she wondered how the two weddings aboard the boat would be handled in inclement weather. There was enough rain in Oregon that this must be a contingency well planned for.

The glass door of the main house was unlocked. Megan entered, calling John's name as she did so, looking for a clock. Lily peered at her from over the top of the sofa, obviously nonplussed to be caught on the furniture. Megan absorbed the details of the room she'd been far too tired to notice the night before, admiring the watercolors on the wall, the shelves of well-worn books, the bronze statue of a tugboat in the corner.

"John?" she called again.

Lily barked.

"You're not too sure about me, are you?" Megan asked the dog, who stared right through her.

Megan finally saw a clock hanging on the wall above a small desk and was shocked to see it was after nine o'clock. They'd overslept!

She hurried down the hall, knocking on and opening doors as she went. One room was filled with stacked boxes, one was a bathroom, another a small room in the process of being paneled with what appeared to be teak. The last opened into what had to be John's room.

A huge four-poster bed sat square in the middle of the room, ivory sheets and comforter tossed aside, empty. An open door to the left revealed a bathroom, equally empty. Megan glanced out the glass doors that opened onto the patio. Nothing.

She walked back down the hall and toward what she figured was the kitchen. This was a large room, too, big on natural wood, tarps covering most of the surfaces, protecting them from spattered paint. A ladder, a closed can of eggshell-white paint, and two cleaned brushes attested to the ongoing process, which seemed to involve the ceiling. One small area nestled between two beams remained to be finished.

Megan finally noticed a note stuck to the refrigerator with a magnet.

"Megan," it began. "Couldn't wake you. There's fresh coffee on the counter. Help yourself to toast or eggs or cereal, sorry about the mess in here. Oh, and there's a few dollars in the sugar bowl behind the toaster—take what you need to get yourself home. John."

Her first feeling was one of alarm—she'd been left behind in a near stranger's home! The second feeling was irritation—how dare he leave her stranded out here in the middle of nowhere! The third feeling was the one that stuck—relief!

She poured herself a cup of coffee, took an old thick coat hanging on a peg by the door and shrugged it on, then went back out on the patio, settling at last on the rock wall. Lily eyed her suspiciously from a hollow beneath a bush. The sky above was heavy with clouds, the river below, a mindless companion intent on its own goal.

After all, there was no rush. John would be gone all day; she could call Mother later. Megan could think of no place she'd rather be than where she already was.

Chapter Four

John glanced at his watch for the third time in as many minutes. He blamed this uncharacteristic fidgetiness on Mrs. Colpepper, who had failed to arrive at the dock and was now late for the loading pier, as well. Danny Borel, grudgingly taking over for Colpepper, was out greeting the first wave of passengers.

As he ran through his checklist, John found his mind wandering to his house, or perhaps more honestly, to the woman he'd left sleeping in his guest house. He'd tried rousing her, banging on the door and calling her name, but short of unlocking the door and dragging her bodily out of bed, he wasn't sure what else he could have done to wake her. It bothered him to know she was there alone. Of course it did! After all, she was a virtual stranger. Maybe she'd rob him blind or trash his house.

Even John had to smile at himself as these irrational thoughts scampered around inside his head.

Danny Borel opened the wheelhouse door and stepped inside. Foggy Dew, apparently sensing her chance to escape the damp oppression of the outside, darted between his legs. "What's wrong with you?" he said at once.

John shook his head. "Nothing is wrong with me."

"You're scowling."

"It's that woman. Where in the hell is she?"

"Colpepper?"

"Of course, Colpepper! What other woman is there?"

Danny smiled. "There's that pretty bride who kicked you out of your cabin, for one. How'd you ever get her off the boat?"

John gestured vaguely toward the dock. "After a while, she came to her senses and left."

"After dark? You didn't let her walk away alone, did you?"

"I'm not a complete idiot," John said impatiently. "I gave her a ride. Listen, did Colpepper say anything to you about taking a day off?"

"No, but it's no secret she was awfully upset."

"She's always threatening to quit," John sputtered.

Danny's eyes grew wide. "She threatened to quit?"

"It doesn't matter. She always comes back."

"Well, maybe this time she won't."

John glanced out the window and saw a sea of black umbrellas lining the rail. As he stared, a man tipped his umbrella back so that John could see him clearly. A frown, which looked as though it might be a permanent feature, dominated his face. A woman standing next to him turned at that moment and John saw that she, too, wore a dour expression. "Is *that* the wedding party?"

Danny, looking over John's shoulder, said, "Yep. Happy-looking group, aren't they?"

"They look like they're going to a funeral, not a wedding."

Danny sighed. "They're a little…upset…that Colpepper wasn't here to greet them. I wouldn't turn my back on them if I were you. By the way, did Colpepper leave any papers up here?''

"Check her office.''

"I did. Zippola. I was hoping you had something.''

"Like what?''

"Like those forms everyone fills out. I know it's just a cake and punch reception—''

"What else do you need to know?''

"Their names would be nice.''

John opened his drawer, searching for aspirin. "You don't know their names?''

"You're the captain,'' Danny said succinctly. "You're the one who was supposed to go to the rehearsal.''

No aspirin. John slammed the drawer. "I'm sorry, Dan, I don't have the slightest idea what their names are. You're going to have to find out for me.''

"Get Colpepper back,'' Danny said from the door. "Beg. Grovel. I don't care, just get her back.''

John gently removed Foggy Dew from her perch atop his seat, tucked her beneath his arm and absently scratched her between the ears, frowning at the river, thinking. No doubt about it—females, be they young or old, plain or pretty, feline or human, were just plain trouble....

Rain pelted the kitchen window as Megan washed her coffee cup and John's breakfast dishes, figuring it was the least she could do. Besides, little chores like this kept her from thinking too much about what had happened yesterday.

She was startled when Lily barked from the living room. Drying her hands on a dish towel, Megan hurried through the house to see what had upset the dog. Lily was standing by the front door issuing a deep woof every few seconds.

Megan looked through the glass panel in time to see a woman, all but obscured by a sizable umbrella, trotting down the path. She opened the door as the woman got into a white station wagon with the engine running. The umbrella closed right before the door did. The car was out of the driveway before Megan could yell. Lily barked again, this time from the end of the path.

Hmm—

A girlfriend? John's ex-wife? Megan hadn't been able to see her face and she was disappointed to have failed to get a glimpse of the kind of woman John might be attracted to. She was about to reenter the house when she spied a bound stack of papers on the redwood bench next to the door. The top paper was pocked with fresh raindrops. She leaned down and saw that it was a note addressed to John, signed "Agnes Colpepper." Shamelessly, she read it.

"Consider this my formal resignation. Here is the event schedule for the next six weeks. I expect my back pay to be sent to the usual address. Don't forget you owe me eight hours overtime. If you want to apologize, call me."

Megan closed the heavy door behind her. So, the female visitor had been Mrs. Colpepper and this was the way she had chosen to quit her job! Did the papers being delivered to the house mean that John wasn't even aware he'd lost his events coordinator? Did that mean he was out there on the river, in the rain, running the whole show by himself? And hadn't he mentioned that there were two weddings that day?

A scratching noise at the door roused Megan from speculative thoughts. She flung it open to find that she'd locked Lily outside. With a withering glance, the dog made a beeline for the rug in front of the cold fireplace.

Megan stared at the house around her as she realized John's predicament was her fault. If she hadn't pushed Robert overboard, Mrs. Colpepper wouldn't have had a fit and quit. Megan deposited the stack of papers on the dining-room table and went back into the kitchen, but within seconds, retraced her steps.

It's none of your business, she told herself, but in a way it was.

She untied the strings and removed the note. At first, as she scanned sheet after sheet, she stood, but after a while, she pulled out a chair and sat. Twenty minutes into it, she decided that this job wasn't that much different from what she did—what she used to do—at the hospital, with the exception that this job didn't require asking anyone for money to fund a new wing or to launch some innovative program. Thirty minutes into it, she frowned.

There were forms for each event, which ranged from birthday celebrations to weddings, business parties to private sight-seeing trips. For the weddings, each bride filled out a multipage form listing all the details of her ceremony and reception aboard the *Ruby Rose*. Megan was familiar with this routine because she herself had done this so recently. The morning ceremony planned for that day was a simple one. The afternoon affair seemed to be just about as fancy as Megan's own aborted wedding, and tears of loss filled her eyes.

For a moment she thought of Robert, of the good times they'd shared and the not-so-good. Where was he right at that moment? Was he regretting his impulsive behavior, was he ruminating over what he had lost, and if he did and if he was, did it matter to her?

She wasn't sure if her tears were regret or relief, but she shook her head defiantly. She made a vow right there and then: she would not continue to be a damsel in distress. The role was tedious and distasteful and she was through with it.

She thought of John Vermont, of his cool, steady gaze and his broad shoulders. He was shy and gruff and obviously desperate to get her out of his life; and that's what she needed to be doing—getting out of his life.

As she attempted to restack the papers in order, a few words penciled on one of the two weddings slated for that very day caught her eye. "Severe allergy to egg whites," it said. "Omit from *every* dish." Attached by paper clip was the menu. This bride had chosen a varied and elegant repast and Megan couldn't help but wonder how many of the dishes were made with ingredients that included egg whites. Pasta? Salads with a mayonnaise base? Breads with an egg wash? If the bride had made the request, would the groom then relax and believe each food to be safe for his consumption? What if they weren't? Had the allergy notation been lost in the shuffle? If the forms were here in John's house, had the onboard caterers even seen the warning?

For some time she drummed her fingers on the tabletop, thinking. At last she looked through the papers until she found the stern-wheeler's phone number. Still, she paused, weighing the pros and cons of sticking her nose in where it didn't belong. However, once the question had been raised, how could she not respond? What if the poor groom went into anaphylactic shock while they were halfway down the river? What would happen to him—and to John Vermont—then?

What kind of ding-a-ling quit in this way, sneaking around like a thief, leaving notes? No wonder John had sounded exasperated when he'd spoken of Mrs. Colpepper! Perhaps she did her job well enough, but after all, coordinating the events for the stern-wheeler couldn't be that hard. In fact, from what Megan had seen, it looked easy…and fun.

In the end, Megan discovered there was really no decision to be made; there was just too much at stake.

By the time John closed the truck door behind him and dashed between raindrops to his front door, he was weary from head to toe. The day had been a slice of hell and if he ever got his hands on Agnes Colpepper, he fully planned on wringing her neck. At least she'd had the decency to call the boat and avert disaster, and he supposed he should be thankful for that.

As usual, when he wasn't shepherding wayward brides around, he'd changed clothes at the ship, leaving his wool jacket and navy slacks hanging in a locker, donning instead jeans and a flannel shirt covered with a hooded rain jacket.

The light was on in the entryway. Obviously, Megan hadn't switched it off when she left. He took off his jacket and hung it on a rack, profoundly glad to be home for fourteen hours, half of which he'd spend asleep. The house felt deserted and he told himself how glad he was that Megan Morison had departed, how very nice it was to be back to normal, alone again. In the next second it finally occurred to him that Lily hadn't greeted him at the door, desperate to go outside for a bathroom break.

Odd.

A tantalizing smell emanating from the kitchen drew his attention, and he walked quickly toward the back of the house, wondering if Megan had left something on the stove, wondering what kind of disaster awaited him.

Lily got to her feet when he entered the kitchen and, wagging her tail, licked his hand. The reason she wasn't anxious to go outside was readily apparent by the raindrops that covered her back. Megan must have let the dog out before she'd left, which couldn't have been long ago. In fact, judging from the simmering pan of sauce that bubbled on a back burner, he realized he must have just missed her. He interpreted the sudden stab in his stomach as a hunger pang.

That's when he noticed that the ladder, drop cloths, and paint cans that had decorated the place for more than a month were gone. His gaze went to the ceiling, where he discovered the remaining section now as white as all the rest, and he cast a critical once-over to search for imperfections, annoyed that the woman had had the gall to paint his ceiling.

Despite a careful search, he found no excess paint on the beams, no brush marks—the whole thing was done as methodically as the rest of the ceiling. It was a mystery to him as to why she had gone to all the trouble and he briefly searched for a note. Lily whined seconds before John heard a bang that caused him to twist around toward the back door.

She blew into the kitchen like a breath of fresh air, hands full of herbs, blond hair tousled and damp, face radiant from the cool rain. She grinned when she saw him, and he fought the urge to grin back. What in the hell was she doing at his house, acting like she owned the place!

With one foot, Megan closed the door behind her. "I bet you're surprised to see me," she said.

"You could say that."

Passing by him, she walked to the sink and picked through the few herbs that had managed to live through the winter. It seemed to John that she avoided looking at him. It also seemed reasonable to him that she explain why she was still at his house, but she quietly chopped up some sickly looking parsley and oregano and, passing him again, dropped them into the saucepan.

He stood by silently watching as she filled another pan with water and put it on to boil, as she absently stirred the sauce with a wooden spoon. He noticed she was wearing his apron, the green-and-white-striped one he wore on rare occasions. It looked good on her. Hell, face it, everything looked good on her. He frowned.

"I can see you're…upset to find me here, but honestly, John, I couldn't leave without expressing my thanks."

He gestured to the ceiling with a toss of his head. "Painting my house was thanks enough."

"Oh, that," she said with a nervous laugh and a shrug. "I like to paint."

He heard himself snap, "Did you clean the brushes? They were some of my best brushes—"

She smiled faintly. "Of course I cleaned your brushes." Biting her lip, she added, "I hope you like Italian food. With what little you keep on hand around here, it was all I could come up with."

"You shouldn't have bothered," he said. "I don't usually eat dinner at the house. Most of the time I stop on my way home."

"Then you've already eaten," she said, eyes downcast.

"Ah…no," he admitted. And why was that? Why had he bypassed his favorite haunt, the River Rat, and hurried back to his cold, empty house, which turned out to be not so cold and not so empty after all?

"Good," she said.

He pulled a stool out from the bar and perched on the edge of it. His turncoat dog was sitting by Megan's legs, waiting, John knew, for a handout. His initial irritation at finding this woman in the house was fading, which annoyed him. She dumped a package of fettuccine, which had been around since Betsy left, into the water.

He studied her closely for signs of impending tears, but found none. Was she over Winslow so fast or was she putting on a brave front? More to the point, why was she still here and how did he go about getting rid of her without opening the floodgates?

Eventually, she set a plate in front of him and he decided that since she'd fixed it, he might as well eat. He was startled to discover she was a very good cook. For some reason, he'd thought she'd be lousy in the kitchen.

"Actually," she said, twirling long noodles around her fork and looking at him from beneath her lashes, "wanting to thank you for all you've done for me wasn't the only reason I stayed."

Irrationally, his heart began to beat faster. "It's not?"

She shook her head. He hadn't once seen her pat her hair or in any other way try to fix herself up after coming inside from the windy rain. He liked that. He'd never understood why so many women tossed, stroked and fondled their tresses. Hers were messy in a beguiling kind of way, which fit her. Again she smiled, her lips a perfect bow shape, dimples he hadn't noticed before popping out on either side of her mouth. He wondered if for some reason he couldn't fathom she was about to come on to him. Maybe it was an instinct to her, maybe having lost one rich jerk, she was desperate to hook up with another.

"I wanted to know how it went today. Out on the boat, I mean. Without Mrs. Colpepper."

John furrowed his brow. "How did you know Colpepper didn't show up?"

She scooted off the stool and disappeared into the formal dining area, returning in seconds with a stack of papers tied with a string. She set it in front of him and read the note Colpepper had written. Swearing, he thumped his fist on the counter so hard it rattled his abandoned fork against the china plate. "That damn woman!" he roared. "Like hell I'll call her!"

She stared at him, silent.

"You should have seen the morning wedding. Danny tried everything under the sun to lighten those people up but it was without a doubt the most morose ceremony I've ever officiated. Why would she do this to me?"

"Maybe she was afraid to face you," Megan said.

He turned incredulous eyes to her. "Afraid to face me? Why on earth would you think that?"

She tried to hide a smile behind her napkin, but he saw it all the same. He snarled some and added, "Well, at least she called the boat and warned us about the food allergy. It was too late to change everything, but Cook was able to prepare an alternate feast for the happy couple, which they fed to each other with grins on their silly faces. Better late than never, I guess."

Megan cleared her throat. "She didn't call. I did."

He'd untied the string and was in the process of finding

that Colpepper had left him with a big old mess when Megan's statement sank in and he looked up at her. "What?"

"Mrs. Colpepper left these papers early this morning. I'm nosy, so I read the note, and I'm curious, so I looked through the papers. When I saw that notation about the egg allergy I decided it was better to err on the side of caution, so I called your galley."

"And pretended to be Agnes Colpepper?"

She shrugged again. "Assumptions were made, which I let stand."

"Are you telling me that Agnes Colpepper quit without telling anyone about this man's allergy?"

"It appears so."

He was stunned. "Hell, I can understand her wanting to get back at me for all her imagined slights, but that poor guy today told me what happens to him—he swells up like a blowfish. Everywhere, mind you, including his throat, which cuts off his breathing. I would have had to call the coast guard and request a helicopter evacuation and then, if he hadn't died, he would have sued me. Wait until I get my hands on that blasted woman!"

Tirade delivered, it occurred to John he hadn't thanked Megan, who *had* saved the day. But for her curiosity and then her follow-through, he'd have a sick man on his conscience and a lawsuit on his hands. He said, "Thanks, Megan. I owe you one."

She answered him with another smile, which flickered on and off like a defective lightbulb. Was she nervous? About what? She finally said, "Actually, John, I think I know how you can repay me."

He pushed the annoying papers aside. Despite his knowledge that this was a woman attracted by money, the thought that she was now going to put the bite on him was extremely disappointing. With a sigh, he said, "How much?"

She turned quizzical eyes on him. "How much what?"

Maybe he'd misjudged her. He waved an impatient hand and said, "Never mind. Go on with what you were saying."

She cleared her throat. "Give me Colpepper's job for a few weeks."

John leaned forward. Had he heard her right? "Her job?" he squeaked.

"I can do it, I know I can," she said, her blue eyes suffused with passion. "The business end of it is far less complicated than what I do—what I did—at the hospital. Since I just organized my own wedding, I wouldn't have any trouble with that end of it. As for the other events, well, I've organized and hosted more than my share of fund-raisers. I can do it, John."

He stared at her. All he could think was that, having ruined one lucrative prospect, she was now setting her sights on him. Why else had she painted his kitchen and fixed him dinner? Hell, she'd even wheedled her way into the dog's affection!

"It's a simple business proposition," she said, as though sensing the direction of his thoughts.

That was another thing—how could she even consider getting back aboard his boat after yesterday's fiasco? Obviously she hadn't thought this through. He said, "It's not the business side of it I'm thinking about."

She stared at him a second before responding. "What then?"

Did she have to ask? He didn't want to hurt her feelings...

"What are you trying to say?" she persisted. "Come on, just spit it out."

If that's the way she wanted it, that's the way it would be. He said, "I was thinking about how you'd *feel*."

"How I would *feel* about what?"

She could not be this obtuse! "About getting back on

my boat," he said. "The same boat you were supposed to
be married on, only you didn't, and if you took this job,
you'd have to help other people do the very same thing
you mucked up yourself."

There! He'd stated his case. He kind of wished he'd
thought of different words to express himself but, oh, well,
it was done. Surely now she'd break into tears and back
away from this absurd idea.

She put her hands on either side of her plate and leaned
toward him. "So, how do *you* handle it?"

"Me?"

"Yeah, you. You, the divorced man, standing up there
day after day uniting people in wedded bliss, a bliss you
were unable to attain or at least, to sustain. Must really get
to you, huh?"

"Now wait just a second. *I* am not the issue."

"Nor am *I*. This is a job. Sure, my wedding plans were
bungled, but that doesn't mean I can't handle other people's happiness."

He pulled out contingency plan two, which he'd just
devised. "I thought you were going to try to get your old
job back."

She rubbed the back of her neck. "I called this afternoon. They hired someone else the day after I left. I might
as well admit to you that I was embarrassed to beg for my
old job back, even if I thought there was a chance they'd
give it to me. It's time for me to move on."

Contingency plan three, which was still so new the paint
was wet, leaped to his tongue. "As a matter of fact, Megan, I'm currently looking for a replacement for my own
position. In other words, with any luck, I won't be captain
of the stern-wheeler for many more trips."

She shrugged. "I can work with *anyone,*" she said, her
voice steady and her eyes bright.

He politely refrained from pointing out she'd sent her
fiancé over the railing twice. "I called today and added

the job of consultant to the listing," he added, watching her face.

She smiled at him. "If someone better comes along, I'll understand. Meanwhile, you won't have to go it alone. You won't be sorry you hired me, John. I'm very good at what I do."

He stared at her, surprised to discover he was irritated by her abundant confidence. On the other hand, there was a school outing planned for the next day as well as a wedding.... The thought of facing them alone with only Danny for help made him break out in a cold sweat. Here, sitting across from him, was his salvation, and yet he hesitated.

"Besides," she added, "if you give me the job then I'll be able to pay you rent for the use of your guest house."

She wanted to live here, at his house!

"That's out of the question."

"Why?"

He stared at her before mumbling, "Well...because."

"Think about it before you rule it out," she said, her voice painfully calm. "If you want, our paths would never have to cross."

"But—"

"On the other hand," she added as she glanced at his empty plate, "if you'd like, I could do the cooking."

Although his mind was spinning like a top, he didn't say anything.

"I'll retrieve my car from Mom's garage so you won't have to drive me anywhere. There's a shelf in the guest house above an outlet that looks as though it's wired for a hot plate and there's a tiny refrigerator in the corner."

"I lived in there while I built this house," John explained.

"I could live there, too," Megan said quietly. "For a little while. Until you find the person you want to take over Mrs. Colpepper's job and I figure out what I want to do next. Then I'd quit the job and leave your house."

She astounded him. Part of him said that allowing her a toehold in his home was stupid, stupid, stupid. She was a self-confessed gold digger. Another part of him said, Don't be a fool, she's a bargain and a half…she can herd everyone around on the boat, she can paint, hell, she can even pinch-hit when Cook needs a hand!

And it was nice sitting across the counter from her….

This last thought made him blink. He said, "*If* we do this, it would be business only."

She looked a mite offended. Aha! He'd come close to exposing her real motives! She said, her voice brisk, "That goes without saying."

"The job doesn't pay much," he added cautiously.

"I don't need much."

Still he stared at her even though she'd dropped her gaze onto her folded hands. He finally said, "You're still hiding."

She raised her head. "No—"

"Sure you are. Have you called your mother or faced Winslow?"

"I don't see that it's any concern of yours how I handle my family—" she began, but he interrupted.

"If you're going to use my boat and my house as a hideout, I think I have the right to know."

Lifting a finger, she said, "Wait a second. You just said that our relationship is to be strictly business. My family is off-limits."

"Then the answer is no thanks, I'll hire someone out of the paper." He folded his arms across his chest, pretty pleased with himself for having stuck to his guns, refusing to think about the fact that a previous ad he'd placed in the paper had yielded Mrs. Colpepper. It didn't matter— if Megan thought she was going to run right over the top of him, she was sorely mistaken.

She sighed deeply and cast him an annoyed frown. "I called Robert's house and left a message on his answering machine. My mother is picking me up here in about ten minutes and giving me a ride back to her place so I can retrieve my car and clothes and get started on the odious job of returning wedding presents.'' An ironic glint sparked her eyes as she added, ''*If,* of course, this all meets your approval.''

John nodded feebly. He felt like a world-class busybody. He heard himself say, ''If I say no to this idea of yours, where will you go, what will you do?''

She shrugged. ''I'll think of something. That's not your problem.'' She smiled and sighed at the same time. Her eyes a little dreamy, she added, ''All I want from you is a job and a place to stay while I think things through. I'll pay my own way. I think that out on your boat, out on the water, I'll find respite and…peace.''

Peace? John thought of all the odd jobs she'd discover went with the territory, jobs that had little or nothing to do with staging fancy weddings. Painting trim, mopping decks, dusting, tidying, running errands, soothing the sometime cantankerous public…was she prepared for such an unromantic workload? It might be interesting to watch what happened when reality got in the way of her fantasies.

Besides, she was just a wisp of a girl, easy enough for him to guard against. Knowing what she was should protect him. Knowing her values and goals would help offset the twinkle in her big blue eyes, the way she had of saying the most startling things as though they were entirely reasonable, the way she wore his green-and-white apron, the sight of her in his kitchen, filling the room with the good smells of her cooking, the warmth of her laughter, her presence.

''Just business,'' he repeated.

She rolled her eyes. ''Oh, for heaven's sake. Are you going to hire me or not?''

Taking a deep breath, knowing in the back of his head

that he was probably going to regret this decision, he nevertheless put out a hand and said, "The job is yours."

She beamed with satisfaction as she put her smaller, softer hand into his and met his gaze. "You won't regret it," she assured him. "I'll be no trouble. All business, just like you said, I promise."

"Hmm. Well, after I wash the dishes, I'll fill you in on a few details of the operation."

"Then I'll start tomorrow," she said. "I have so many ideas. Really, John, I don't think Agnes Colpepper fully capitalized on all the opportunities. For instance, do you have disposable cameras aboard?"

"Ah, no…"

"See what I mean? Do you have any idea how many people forget to bring a camera? Why don't we have some for sale?"

"We?" he croaked, fighting off a wave of terror. She wasn't going to *change* things, was she? Not immediately, anyway. Wait! He was the boss. Changes would have to go through him, not around him.

She studied him for a second and he tried to adjust his face, to erase from his features the panic her straightforwardness induced in him. "You," she said at last. A slight hesitation was followed by a toss of her head and obvious redetermination. "I was also thinking about public cruises and weekend brunches."

"Brunches," he said woodenly.

"Of course. You have a big galley aboard, right?"

"Yes…"

"You could hire additional help. Not right away, of course."

"Of course," he said with a twisted smile. As she waxed poetic about food service, once again wearing her I-can-conquer-the-world face, the doorbell rang.

Her voice petered out; she bit her lip and met his gaze. "That's got to be my mother," she said, her voice suddenly filled with what sounded like dread. "John, I should warn you. Sometimes Mom can say...well, she can be a little—"

He cut her off by standing. "You forget I've met your mother. I can handle her."

"Famous last words," she mumbled.

Chapter Five

As John answered the front door, Megan put on her rain-coat and searched for her purse, which she could have sworn she'd left on the shelf by the kitchen door. The purse was nowhere in sight, which meant it must be out in the guest house. For a second she paused, door half open, as she heard her mother's high-pitched voice and the deeper tones of Uncle Adrian. She might have known the two of them would form a united front!

Anxious to usher her family away from John's house before they said or did something to embarrass her, she sprinted through the drizzle. The guest house yielded the purse, which Megan slung over her shoulder as she raced back, still hopeful she could run interference. No such luck.

All three of them were standing in the entryway. Me-gan's mother, who was all of five foot two inches, was dwarfed by the two men, though Uncle Adrian was almost as wide around as he was tall. All three of them turned to look at Megan as she stepped into the living room. Her gaze went first to John, whose eyes were snapping, then to Uncle Adrian, who seemed amused by something, and lastly to her mother, who rushed forward and grabbed both of Megan's hands.

"Honey, I've been worried sick about you!" Glancing briefly over her shoulder at John, she added, "Are you all right?"

"Of course I'm all right," Megan said as she self-consciously shrugged her hands away. "Why wouldn't I be all right?"

"You were so upset on the phone—"

"No, I wasn't upset—"

"And I was just telling this…man…what Robert said when I called him."

"Oh, Mother, tell me you didn't call Robert."

"Well, of course I did," Megan's mother said. "He and I have been in constant contact since that unfortunate accident on the boat."

"I pushed him over the side. It wasn't exactly an accident."

"Now, honey, don't act like this. You know how anxious I am that you two get back together." She looked at John again and added, "Megan has an opportunity to marry a very important man. I didn't tell him that she was shacked up here. Heaven only knows what he'll say—"

"Mother!"

John said, his voice tight, "For the *second* time, Mrs. Morison, we are not 'shacked up.'"

"You don't have to defend me," Megan said.

He met her gaze with those piercing blue eyes and shook his head. "I'm not defending *you*, I'm defending *me*."

Uncle Adrian touched Megan's mother's arm. "Lori—"

Lori Morison ignored her brother. "Robert will take care of Megan and provide for her. She couldn't ask for anyone better than Robert Winslow. She needs to concentrate on getting him back."

"I don't believe this," Megan remarked. "You're talk-

ing about me as though I'm twelve years old and not even
in the room.''

Uncle Adrian groaned. ''Lori, you've said enough. This
man is—''

''I just want him to know what's at stake,'' Lori Morison interrupted. ''Haven't I always said that Robert is the
spitting image of Megan's father? He's perfect for her.''

Megan sighed. ''I have gone way past being humiliated,
Mother. Please, just stop talking.'' She spared John a
glance; he looked as though he wished all his visitors
would spontaneously combust. Addressing her mother
again, she added, ''I know you're disappointed. I know
you wanted Robert for me because you believed he was
best for me, but you're going to have to understand that I
have decided he isn't and, after all, this is my life we're
talking about. At any rate, this isn't the time or the place
for this conversation. John doesn't have the slightest interest in any of it.''

Lori blinked rapidly. ''Who in the world is John?''

Uncle Adrian cleared his throat. ''That's what I've been
trying to tell you since we got here.'' Gesturing at John,
he added, ''This man is John Vermont, the captain of the
stern-wheeler. Don't you recognize him, Lori?''

She narrowed her eyes until recognition dawned. ''Oh.''

''Please,'' Megan said. ''Let's just leave.''

But Lori, as determined and tenacious as a fox terrier,
had her neck craned as she zeroed in on John. ''Why did
you bring my daughter here? Do you have any idea how
this will look to Robert?''

''I don't really give a damn how anything looks to Robert,'' John said, his voice tight.

Lori turned to her daughter. ''If he's not a new boy-
friend, what are you doing at his house? Did you know
this man before the ceremony? What's going on here?''

Megan glanced at John. She yearned to say something
that would put him at ease, but she sensed any further

dialogue would just extend his misery. She took her mother's arm and opened the front door. "Go to the car," she said, gently shoving her mother out onto the porch. Her mother, uttering words of indignity, stomped out into the rain.

Megan paused at the door and looked at John again. He met her gaze and smiled—kind of.

Adrian chuckled as he clapped John's shoulder. "Thanks for watching after our girl." Addressing Megan, he added, "Well, kiddo, no use delaying the inevitable. Let's go."

Megan shook her head. "I'm warning you, Uncle Adrian. I know how you feel about Robert, I know how he bailed out your business, etcetera, etcetera. But I can't—I won't—take this barrage from both you *and* Mother."

Adrian laughed. "Calm down, girl." Looking back at John, his voice suddenly somber, he said, "Funny thing about Robert Winslow's help—it comes with a hefty price tag. My company, debts and all, used to be mine, but now it's his and I'm nothing but a flunky shareholder." He turned his attention back to Megan and added, "So don't fret, honey, I'm not losing sleep over your losing Winslow. That's your mother's department."

As Adrian strode past her, Megan spared one last look at John. In a microsecond she thought of and discarded a dozen things to say, a dozen explanations, settling on a simple, "I'm really sorry about all this."

He nodded curtly, but the knot in his jaw seemed to disappear.

"I don't know where she got all her crazy ideas—"

"It's okay, Megan."

She took a deep breath. "Do I still have a job?"

He seemed to ponder her question before smiling in such a disarming way that she felt rather funny inside. "If your mother doesn't have me arrested for white slavery, you still have a job.''

"And my family is my business?"

He raised both hands. "Absolutely."

She didn't want to leave and she didn't want to too closely examine why she didn't want to leave. Instead she closed the door behind her and trudged through the rain toward the car and inevitable confrontation inside.

John stared at the book that lay open in his lap and tried to concentrate. Steinbeck was one of his favorite authors and *Cannery Row* a much-read favorite, yet John knew he wasn't doing the familiar words justice. It seemed his powers of concentration were nonexistent.

At last he closed the book and rose from his chair. After poking at a smoldering log in the fireplace, he glanced at his watch. Twenty minutes had passed since the last time he'd checked the time. It seemed more like hours than minutes.

Lily, apparently sensing his restlessness, looked at him with her head tilted, her brown eyes big and concerned.

"It's okay, girl," he told her as he leaned down and patted her. She immediately resettled her head on her paws and closed her eyes. John wished he could so easily be reassured.

Where was she?

It was after midnight. He'd long ago delivered an alarm clock and a note to the guest house, leaving them both on the nightstand. The note offered Megan a ride in the morning. He'd left the outside lights on for her—simple courtesy—and then he'd retreated to the main house and locked up for the night. At the last minute, instead of heading down the hall to bed, he'd sat down to read for a few minutes before turning in.

That was two hours ago. *Shouldn't she be back by now?*

He paced across the house and found himself looking

out the big glass door toward the guest house, which was dark and empty. He wasn't sure why he was watching for Megan's return. She was obviously capable of taking care of herself, but the scene with her mother had left him feeling shaken. How he hated scenes!

I just want to talk to her, he told himself, and immediately felt a stab of concern. He rephrased his thought. *I just want to make sure she's okay.* The correction left him feeling twice as uneasy.

It wasn't until her headlights bounced off the rock wall and temporarily illuminated the rain-streaked night that he admitted to himself he'd been thinking that she might not return, that her mother might prevail, that Winslow might get his bride back. This would mean he'd lose an events coordinator. Sure, he'd been unsure about hiring her—hell, he still was. But she was better than nothing and he hated to lose her before she even began to work.

He stepped out of sight as she rushed past his house, her arms full of boxes, a clothes bag slung over one shoulder. He watched—on the sly—as she opened the guest-house door and flicked on the lights, as she stepped inside and was momentarily caught in the act of dropping her belongings on the floor, and then as she closed the door and dashed back to her car for another load.

He had his jacket halfway on, thinking that it was only polite to help her move her things in, when he wondered what she would think of his waiting up for her. What if she asked him why? What in the world would he say? As he dithered, she dashed past him again and once more opened the guest-house door.

John turned his back and shook his head as he took off the jacket. What in the world was he doing standing alone in the dark, in the middle of the night, watching this woman, second-guessing everything he saw and said and felt?

"That woman got me more rattled than I thought," he

told Lily, who had the decency to follow him down the hall to his bedroom without asking him to which woman he referred.

Megan was up before dawn, digging through clothing boxes, unsure what to wear. Agnes Colpepper had dressed up for Megan's wedding—was that expected? But what about the second grade outing scheduled for the morning? She couldn't really picture herself chasing after more than twenty seven-year-olds while dressed in silk.

She finally settled on a long, straight blue skirt, white blouse, and red jacket. Her walking shoes looked silly with the outfit so she chose a pair of blue heels. Next came the ubiquitous raincoat. At the last second, she put a flowing navy blue dress, which had been part of her trousseau, in a garment bag. Draping it over her arm, she ran outside to slip into the truck next to John, who had warned her of his seven o'clock departure in a note she'd found when she came home the night before.

"Morning," he said as she closed the door.

She fastened her seat belt as she looked at him. She was nervous for some reason, shaky even. She should have spent more time eating breakfast and less time obsessing about clothes. She said, "Good morning."

As he backed down his driveway, he added, "Did you sleep well?"

"Yes, fine," she said, which was an out-and-out lie. Truth of the matter was that she'd lain awake half the night worrying about this job and the other half worrying about her future. As a matter of fact, right around three o'clock, she'd had the overwhelming urge to call Robert. Recognizing this sudden desire to hear his voice for what it was—a return to the safety of having a man to watch out for her—she'd resolutely rolled over and finally fallen asleep.

"Nice that it's not raining," he said.

Megan agreed with him by nodding. The stilted conversation just flagged their relationship for what it was—new. They had no past to share, no history on which to build. He didn't know very much about her and she knew even less about him. Without shared memories and experiences, they were reduced to talking about the weather. For some unexplainable reason, this depressed the heck out of her.

I want to know him, she realized as she looked again at his rugged profile. On the heels of this thought came another. *I don't know if I have the heart or the energy to invest in someone I'll know only for a few weeks, maybe a couple of months, someone who has made it quite clear he expects me to get myself pulled together and out of his life sooner rather than later.*

The miles slipped by in silence.

The seven-year-olds were giggly and wiggly, excitement making their voices shrill. They obligingly lined up along the rail as the big boat pulled away from the dock, Megan standing with one group, the teacher and two parent volunteers watching over three other groups.

Before they had come, John had given her a whirlwind tour of the boat, which included parts she'd seen before and some she hadn't. He'd shown her how to use the public address system, where the safety gear was located and introduced her to a small waterproof booklet that would help her announce safety rules and points of interest as they toured the harbor. When the children had arrived, she and Danny Borel had gone over everything with them as John climbed the stairs to the bridge.

John didn't much like groups of people; this much was painfully obvious. He'd mentioned he was looking for another captain for this boat. Megan found it hard to imagine another man wearing that blue uniform the way he did. It seemed to her he was an integral part of the stern-wheeler, as necessary as the paddle that dominated the stern of the vessel or the whistles and horns used as signals when they passed by a freighter.

The children loved the horn and it occurred to Megan that they would equally love a visit to the wheelhouse. As a matter of fact, the more she thought about it, the more certain she became that this must be expected protocol and that John had simply forgotten to mention it. She looked around the deck for Danny to ask him about it, but the good-looking first officer had disappeared into a crowd of coeds who were also taking this trip down the Willamette River, and he was obviously busy.

The teacher, however, thought it was a grand idea, and thus bolstered, Megan took the first group of children— five boys and one girl—up the stairs. "Best behavior," she warned as they followed her.

She paused at John's cabin door, and for a second recalled the panic that had forced her inside that cabin less than forty-eight hours before. Time, doing its warp act, made it seem like weeks, not hours, since she had stood on this very spot with a soggy cat wrapped up in her wedding dress and her fiancé paddling below in the river. And it occurred to her that, far from feeling as though her life was in shambles, she felt invigorated.

"Let's be very polite," she told the kids as they climbed the last flight of stairs.

After a brief knock, she opened the bridge door. John, looking incredibly masculine, stood tall and straight in front of the brass levers that he used to steer the ship, but he turned when he heard the noise seven-year-olds make even when they're trying to be quiet. His eyes grew wide as he looked from the children to Megan.

"What in the world—"

She cut him off. "I thought you might enjoy meeting your passengers, Captain."

He blinked a couple of times. "Well…"

''Don't touch,'' she told a small boy whose hands were dangerously close to an important-looking piece of electronic equipment.

John said, ''Really, Megan…''

The girl clapped her hands together and shrieked, which caused Megan's heart to dive down to the pit of her stomach. John, obviously startled, jerked.

''A kitty!'' the child cried.

Foggy Dew, unfazed by the commotion, sat on a wooden chair, her middle bulging, eyes serene. The kids, led by the little girl, moved as one to pet her. She suffered their attention with a startling amount of composure.

John leaned down to whisper in Megan's ear. After the chill outside, his breath felt warm and inviting and she moved away a bit, not because it felt wrong to have his breath caress her but because it felt right.

''This is not the time to have visitors in the wheelhouse,'' he said softly.

Megan's smile faded. ''It's not?''

''No.''

''When is a good time?''

He looked at her as though she was crazy. 'I don't usually have people up here at all,'' he said.

''Never?''

''Rarely. And never kids.''

''But they're not hurting anything,'' she told him reasonably.

''That's not the point. Now, take them down to the lower deck and ask the cook to hand out orange juice or something.''

''First you have to let the other four groups look around,'' she whispered.

''I most certainly do not—''

''Oh, yes, you do,'' she interrupted. ''Don't you know anything about kids? If you don't let them all have the same opportunity you'll have a mutiny on your hands.''

He seemed to notice for the first time that the children had lost interest in the cat and were now gathered around his legs, looking up at him, listening to their conversation. The girl tugged on the hem of his jacket. "Is there a television up here?"

"Uh...no," he said.

"Then what's that?"

She was pointing at a radar screen. He told her what it was.

A chunky boy, wearing more layers than an onion, asked, "Does the cat have a name?"

"Foggy Dew."

"Why is she so fat?"

"Well, she's going to have kittens."

"Can I have one?"

"Me, too," chimed in the other kids.

"We'll have to see about that," he said, glancing at Megan.

She shrugged apologetically, wondering if he had any idea how delightful he looked surrounded by little kids.

The girl said, "Can I drive the boat?"

Another of the boys, a towhead with giant brown eyes, said, "Can I toot the horn?"

"Me, too!" This from everyone else.

Megan watched as one by one, John allowed the children a short blast on the horn. Then, amid massive goodbyes directed at Captain Vermont and the cat, the children were ready to leave.

"I'll get the next group," she said as she herded the kids out the door.

He shook his head.

"Really, John, don't you see, you can't not let the other kids come up here..."

"I know," he said with a sigh. Fixing her with a laser-like stare, he added, "Rest assured, you are going to pay for this."

His words, which surely must have been in jest, made a shiver run up her spine and tingle the roots of her hair. She cast him a blinding smile. "Take it out of my paycheck," she quipped.

"It's going to cost you a lot more than money," he mumbled, which caused another shiver as Megan's imagination ran rampant. It was all she could do to walk down the stairs without stumbling.

As tiring as the morning was, however, it didn't hold a candle to the afternoon. The morning had been hectic and exhausting and fun. The afternoon was emotionally wrenching and she couldn't even let it show because John had warned her that it would be like this and she wasn't about to give him the satisfaction of discovering he was right.

The bride was young and fresh in her satin gown; the groom, handsome and adoring. Together, they looked like the ideal couple. As they gazed lovingly into each other's eyes while John recited the ceremony in his deep voice, Megan worked at keeping her lower lip from trembling and tears from running down her cheeks. Her eyes were moist, however; she couldn't help it, for the two promised to love each other forever without a second's hesitation, without a backward glance, without a pause. When John pronounced them husband and wife, they grinned at each other, they laughed, they kissed…and the dreaded tears made a beeline for Megan's chin.

As the happy newlyweds moved off to be wrapped in the warm circle of their family and friends, Megan noticed John was approaching her. A smile tugged at the corners of his mouth as she hastily dried her face with the tissue she'd thankfully had the foresight to tuck into a pocket.

He stopped right in front of her, glanced down and then looked out at the water. "Got to you a little, didn't it?" he finally murmured.

Megan decided a frontal approach would be the best tack with this unsentimental man. She shrugged and said, "If you like your weddings without a cat as a witness and with no one taking an unscheduled leap into the river, it was okay."

This brought his focus back to her and she smiled. He laughed into his hand, then leaned back against the rail, crossing his long legs at the ankles, staring right into her eyes.

The intensity was too much for her. Megan swept an arm toward the far bank and pointed to the first thing she noticed. "Look at all those red and black boats," she said.

He didn't even look over his shoulder. "They're tugs," he said.

"How do you know without looking?"

"Because we go by them each and every day, because there are eight of them all painted alike, because they're docked less than an eighth of a mile from our home dock and because they used to be mine."

She bit her bottom lip as she turned back around. From his demeanor and his voice, it was obvious that they'd once been important to him and she felt strangely awkward that she'd brought them up.

His melancholy seemed to pass in a blink, however, as his gaze traveled over her form. "That's a beautiful dress," he finally said.

Surprised, flattered, embarrassed, unsure why such an innocent compliment should make her any of the above, she muttered, "Thanks."

"It brings out the color of your eyes."

"I'm glad you like it. I think I'll leave it here and make it my official shipboard dress."

He nodded.

She wanted to talk to him about the morning, about how she'd foisted all those kids on him, about how she was sorry she hadn't checked, but really, hadn't it turned out well? She wanted to apologize again for her mother and the scene at his house the night before. Maybe he'd forgotten all about everything, though, even his threat to make her pay for the kids, so she said nothing. Besides, the photographer was almost finished taking pictures, which meant it was time to check on the reception dinner being laid out below. "I'd better get back to work," she said.

John straightened. "You and me both." Side by side, they walked to the stairs, John taking the flight up, which would return him to the wheelhouse and Megan going down to the lower deck, where the sound of the band, the aroma of the food, and a host of unpleasant memories awaited her.

It began raining as they pulled against the dock. The guests had all been unloaded at the downtown pier and there was nothing left to do now but make a few calls and check over a few papers. As the engine stopped and the ship settled, Megan sat at the desk that had once been Agnes Colpepper's domain and reviewed the upcoming schedule, which included a senior citizens' tour, a double wedding and a birthday party. She made a couple of quick calls to the florist and the bakery for the next day's affair, and finally made a follow-up call to check on the decorations for the dinner-dance several weeks hence. When she was finished, she sat back in her chair and took a deep breath.

The party was for media bigwigs, public relations people, all the kinds of folks she used to work for and with. It was inevitable there would be familiar faces, surely even some that had been at her wedding and witnessed the fiasco. Maybe even Robert!

She rubbed her temples. She didn't want to be anywhere near this party. She wondered if she did all the footwork, all the preparations, if she would actually have to attend the damn thing. She put it on her mental list of things to ask John.

Wiggling bare toes in the plush carpet, she vowed to wear more comfortable shoes the next day. The closet in the coordinator's cabin held nothing but her blue dress draped on the solitary hanger. She'd changed back into skirt and jacket, but she saw no reason why she couldn't store a few personal items here at the ship so that she could at least change into jeans at the end of the day or add a layer when the weather changed.

The office held a beige file cabinet, a long sofa covered in nubby tan tweed and a mahogany desk with a pair of chairs facing it. The room had none of the nautical appeal of John's cabin. If she was going to stay awhile, she thought, she'd hang a few appropriate paintings, add a couple of throw pillows to the sofa, place fresh flowers here and there. As it was, the place looked temporary, which reminded her that that was exactly what it was—a temporary place for her to do business while she figured out the next step of her life.

Tonight, on their way home, she would ask John to stop at a department store so she could buy herself a pair of deck shoes—the leather kind with leather laces and nonslip soles. She also wanted to find a few of those disposable cameras to have on hand—one of the parent volunteers that morning had been bereft because she had forgotten her camera and Megan had thought to herself, *I knew it!*

She found herself staring out the ample porthole. The air had grown noticeably colder as the day progressed. Slanting rain was all she could see, that and a gray sky. She was sick of the rain and fervently hoped summer would be hot and dry and would come early! In her mind's eye, she saw a summer of evening cruises, a band playing, dancing under the stars while the lights of Portland twinkled on all sides. Strong, masculine arms, rough wool under a soft cheek, the smells of the river and woodsy after-shave, the intense hue of the heavens above....

A soft knock was followed by John peeking into the cabin. "Ready to go?"

With a start, she realized her little daydream had included John. It was his wool jacket, his arms. She closed the folder abruptly and put it in the second drawer. "I'm ready," she said.

She'd kicked off her heels and now struggled to put them on a pair of feet that had taken the opportunity to swell. At last, carrying the shoes in one hand, she crossed the cabin barefoot, which brought a smile to John's mouth.

He'd changed into jeans and a waterproof jacket, which made him look less official and a lot younger. His dark hair was damp as though he'd been out in the rain. His large hands held her raincoat for her, then the door.

They went down the stairs to the main deck, which was cold and wet under Megan's bare feet. John caught her arm as she slipped on a patch of slick paint.

"Thanks," she said. She looked down at the spot, which wasn't roughed up with grit in the paint like the rest of the deck and added, "Maybe that should be fixed before someone breaks their neck."

"We're waiting for this infernal rain to stop, then we're going to repaint all the decks," he informed her. He added, "I'll get Danny to mend it temporarily, though. You can help him, it'll be good experience for you. For now, maybe you'd better put your shoes on."

"I can't. My feet are feeling rebellious. They've gone on strike."

"You can't walk on that old pier without shoes," he said as they approached the gangplank.

Good point. Sighing, she bent to force the issue when, to her shock, John swept her off her feet.

"Wait a second," she cried as she flung her arms around his neck.

"I'll just give you a ride to the truck," he said, his voice calm and reasonable. "It's no bother."

She was going to protest, but it was wonderful being held in his arms, their faces almost nose to nose. Besides, she reasoned, there wasn't much chance that she'd ever get those rotten shoes back on her feet anyway.

"Just don't drop me," she warned him.

"I'll try not to," he said as he maneuvered his way down the gangplank.

Actually, she had no fear that he would. His grip was too tight, his arms too strong. She had the strangest feeling he could carry her to the ends of the earth—and the equally odd and totally alarming feeling that she would very much enjoy the ride!

As he stepped off the gangplank, Megan wrenched her gaze away from the enticing view of his lower jaw and looked down at the dock. It was splintery and dark with spilled oil and creosote. Some of the gaps between the boards were wide enough to swallow a leg all the way up to a knee. Far below, the harbor water sloshed against the rocky bank as the wake of a passing freighter came to shore.

"This dock looks as though a stiff wind could blow it over," she said to his chin.

"Wind, no. But a flood might take the whole thing downriver."

"Why don't you move the boat?"

"Premium dock space is hard to find. That's why we rent a pier downtown to load and unload our passengers," he explained, grunting as he stepped over a particularly wide gap. Looking down at her, grinning, he added, "You're heavier than you look."

She knew smooth pavement awaited them on the other side of the abandoned building just a few yards ahead. She said, "That is not a very chivalrous thing to say. Besides, maybe you just haven't been eating your spinach."

"I'll have you know I'm very conscientious about all my food groups," he said, grinding to a halt under the eaves of the building. As the tin roof above them exploded under the assault of raindrops, they exchanged amused smiles until his seemed to slip away like a wistful sigh and the expression in his eyes changed. Water dripped from his ears and jaw. Megan blinked the moisture out of her eyes, took a shallow breath, and waited.

She would have been okay if he'd kept walking or talking or anything but just standing there looking at her as though he'd never seen her before. The wide open space suddenly seemed stuffy, as though there wasn't enough oxygen around, as though there never could be. The tension between them built as each microsecond passed until it was palatable. On impulse, pure and simple, she threw caution to the wind and did what every instinct in her body screamed at her to do—she reached up slightly and kissed his lips.

He drew back, surprise flickering in the depths of his eyes. She intended to smile to let him know this wasn't an overt act of seduction, but before she could put her mouth to this purpose, he'd claimed it with his own.

His kiss was different than her friendly peck. The man put his heart and soul into the matter and it was impossible for Megan not to respond in kind. As his arms tightened around her legs and torso, she lost herself for a moment in a delightful haze of pure sensuality.

And then it was over. She managed to produce the smile at last, but it was one of awe as well as reassurance. She had never, ever, been kissed like that before. Not ever.

John, however, looked mortified, as though his reaction to her had shocked him. In fact, he looked so upset that she felt a fluttering of impatience.

"You can put me down," she said.

He put her down. By now, Megan's feet were almost

numb and she stumbled a little. He caught her arm and steadied her.

She cast him a quick peek from the corners of her eyes as she straightened her skirt. He was still staring. She said, "For heaven's sake, John, say something."

Her libido shot skyward as he laughed softly, rubbed his mouth with the back of his hand and stared at her with smoldering eyes. "You threw me for a loop," he said at last.

"Me?"

"Kissing me," he said. "I wasn't expecting it."

Her libido ebbed as her frustration grew. "You've got to be kidding."

"What?"

"You started it."

"Me?"

"Don't look so innocent, John Vermont. You did it with your eyes. The way you were looking at me. Come on, admit it. Besides, my kiss was nothing, it was yours that got carried away."

He shook his head. "This is the very thing I was afraid of."

She tried to put her shoes on. Though her feet were no longer swollen, they were now so cold and wet that it was slow going. She said, "Oh, I get it. You're worried about the business-only policy."

"That was our agreement."

Leaning against the building, standing on one bare foot while she tugged the shoe on the other, she said, "Then don't go around carrying me and looking at me like you want to ravish me."

"Is that what I was doing?"

His voice sounded annoyed. Good. Smiling, she said, "That's what you were doing."

"That was not my intention."

"Hmm."

"And I think we should just forget it ever happened."

"Forget what happened?"

He took a deep breath. "Do your shoes fit now?"

She stopped struggling with the miserable things. "No, they do not fit now. I can walk, however." Without waiting for a reply, she rounded the corner of the building. Out of the shelter of the eaves, she was instantly bombarded by the full force of the rain and, head down, she made a mad dash for John's truck.

All forward progress came to an abrupt halt when she ran smack into a man in a raincoat who was running in the other direction. They both gasped in surprise. She felt two hands grab her shoulders and hold her at arm's length.

"Robert!"

John stopped right behind her. She heard him mutter, "Great."

Completely ignoring John, Robert said, "Meg, enough is enough." His grip was tight, his face urgent. "It's time for you to start acting like a grown woman and come back with me."

Megan glanced over her shoulder at John's face, which was impossible to read. The rain beat against all three of them, plastering their hair to their heads, running down their faces and coats, drenching them to the skin. Megan's feet were freezing.

She shook her head.

Chapter Six

Megan watched in amazement as Robert's posture softened, as his eyes took on a benevolent glow and he released his grip. His expression turned genteel, patient, and he smiled at her. She'd seen him compose himself this way before, only she had never recognized it as an act intended to disarm an opponent...in this case, her. He ran a hand—browned, she knew, in a tanning salon—through his wet hair.

"Meg, you know I don't like to lose anything I've invested my time and money in," he said softly. "Come back to my place and let's work out a compromise."

"I've asked you time and time again not to call me Meg. Is it really so hard to remember?"

"Honey—"

"Don't 'honey' me."

"Listen, I've thought it through. We'll tell people you were nervous."

"No—"

"And that you overreacted when I told you about the

prenuptial agreement. By now, surely, you've realized how necessary it is for a man like me to protect himself—"

"From a woman like me," she said.

He patted her damp cheek. "Now, Meg—Megan—"

She removed his hand from her face with a decisive motion. "Actually, what really threw me for a loop was when you impulsively kicked a defenseless animal into the river to drown."

He shook his head patiently in a way she imagined was supposed to make her feel like a silly, rebellious child. In all honesty, his past condemnation of her had stung, but glory be, all it did now was irritate her. "I guess you are who you are, Robert," she said. "I guess you can't help being a creep."

His eyes grew wide. "You're still mad about that blasted cat?"

"Imagine that!" she said.

"Would it help if I said I wish now I'd never seen the miserable creature much less kicked it?"

"Actually, no, it wouldn't. The only thing that would help now was if you were to turn around and walk away from here and leave me alone."

"Now, *that's* a good idea," John said with feeling.

Robert cast John a withering glance then directed his attention once more to Megan. "Is it true what your mother said? Are you and this…sailor…well, together?"

John's kiss, so indelibly burned into her memory, so recent, so sensual, flooded her imagination and she felt her cheeks grow warm. She could almost feel John tense behind her. She said, "Absolutely not."

"But your mother—"

"Mom is mistaken," Megan interrupted. She would have to have yet *another* heart-to-heart talk with her blabbermouth mother. She added, "John is my employer, nothing more, nothing less."

This time the look Robert gave John was intense.

"You're awfully quiet," he finally snarled. "Don't you have something to say about this?"

Megan was relieved when John laughed. "Actually, I've noticed the lady doesn't need my help when it comes to dealing with you."

This oblique reference to Megan pushing Robert off the stern-wheeler was not lost on Winslow, who shook his fist at John. "She wasn't like this until she came aboard your leaky barge."

For the first time John raised his voice. "Maybe it just took her that long to come to her senses," he said.

"And maybe I'll just sue you for disrupting my wedding!"

"Why don't you do that?"

Megan grasped Robert's arm. "Calm down—" she began, but, tearing his arm away, he cut her off.

"I've had it with you!" he told her, eyes blazing. "You've burned your bridges with me, sweetheart." He took a few steps, then turned back and addressed John, punching the air to emphasize his words. "And I'll see *you* in court!"

"I'll be counting the days!" John called as Winslow stalked back to his sedan.

Megan shook her head again. "Men," she grumbled.

"Hey, don't lump us all in one category."

"You're all macho hotheads."

"I kept my temper—"

"Right up until he dissed your boat," she observed smugly.

"He just went too far," John said with conviction, adding, "I can't believe you were ever in love with that man."

Hugging herself for warmth, Megan agreed. "Neither can I. And I'm sorry you keep getting dragged into my personal affairs."

"Are there any more irate people lurking in the wings waiting to spring out and verbally attack you?" he asked.

"Let's see, we've had my mother and Robert. Uncle Adrian has turned out to be an unexpected ally. I think it's over. I sure hope so."

"Me, too," he said with feeling. "I really don't like...scenes."

She said, "Believe it or not, neither do I." Teeth chattering, feet freezing, she added, "Maybe we should have the brains to get in out of the rain."

He nodded stiffly. Again, he took her arm. She decided her accelerated heartbeat had to do with the fear that Robert might make good his threat and drag John to court. The publicity couldn't be good for a small business.

"That guy is a real jerk," John said, as apparently his thoughts had also returned to Robert Winslow.

"Yes," she said, vowing silently to find a way to protect John from Robert's wounded pride.

John reluctantly got to his feet and walked to his desk to answer a persistent phone. Megan was curled up in his favorite chair with her hands wrapped around a warm mug of cocoa. He'd been relegated to the sofa and both of them—well, all three when you counted Lily—had been gazing into a roaring fire after a simple dinner of soup and crackers. It had been hours since they'd driven home so wet their clothes had left huge water marks on the seat covers, but it seemed the chill was as hard to chase away as the memory of their brief encounter.

The call took the better part of ten minutes but when he replaced the receiver and returned to his chair, it was with the knowledge that a competent-sounding man was going to show up at the stern-wheeler the next day to interview for the job of captain. With any luck, John's stint aboard the *Ruby Rose* might be coming to an end.

"That sounded like an important call," she said after taking a sip of her hot chocolate.

"I may have found my replacement," he said as he propped his slippered feet back on the coffee table.

Her gaze flicked from his face to the fire. Half lit by the orange glow, John couldn't help but notice that she was a study in shadows and contrasts. During the ride home, he'd tried hard to reestablish their friendly relationship, putting the ill-thought kissing incident as far out of his mind as he could. He'd known she would try to get to him and, damn it all, she had. But in all honesty, he'd done his share to help.

"I should go to bed," she said through a yawn, but she didn't move an inch.

Outside, the relentless rain pounded on the roof. It had turned cold and John knew this same rain was producing late snow up in the mountains. He wondered where he'd stowed his skiing gear. He wondered if Megan liked to ski.

This careering back and forth from thinking about her to being wary of her was driving him nuts. She was only a few days away from having planned a future with Robert Winslow and here she was, kissing him. If she hadn't needed work and a place to stay and he hadn't needed a replacement for Agnes Colpepper, they would have said goodbye two days earlier and never seen each other again and he wouldn't be sitting here with his thoughts going back and forth like a Ping Pong ball.

"I can't believe Robert thought he could just waltz back into my life," she said.

He looked up from the fire. "Yeah," he muttered. "Some nerve."

"Good thing he didn't come across us a couple of moments earlier," she added, casting him an amused smile.

Aha, she was referring to the kiss. He knew she wouldn't be able to leave it alone. Well, if she wanted to talk about it, she could just come sit beside him on the sofa and they'd talk. Talking was good. They could get everything out in the open, clear it all up. *Kissing was a mistake,* he'd tell her again. She would have to leave if she couldn't remember this. He wished she would come sit closer so he could tell her this. It seemed kind of counterproductive to actually invite her to sit closer.

"As it was, things were bad enough," she said, shuddering. "If he'd seen us kissing, I know he would have taken it all wrong."

A new thought poked itself into the melee in his head. He'd known men and women who became more interested in a jilted lover after that lover no longer cared for them. Was she now obsessing about Winslow because the imbecile had told her he was through with her?

"I've been thinking about what you said earlier."

He cleared his throat. "What did I say?"

"About Robert. About how you couldn't understand how I'd ever loved a man like him."

See? More talk about Winslow. He inwardly groaned and made a point of looking at his watch.

She set her mug on a side table and scooted around in her chair until she faced him. Her hair had dried kind of curly and she was wearing a black sweater, black leggings and red slippers with rubber soles. Damn, if she didn't look cute. "I think it has to do with my father," she said.

Her father. Okay, he could handle her father.

"He died when I was twelve. Up until that time, life was...wonderful. He was so handsome and so friendly— people adored him. *I* adored him." She smiled wistfully as her thoughts danced through her past. John made himself stop staring into her eyes. Part of the way she got to him was by acting as though she had no idea how she got to him or even that she was getting to him. She was very clever this way.

Resting her chin on her clasped hands, she added, "He called me Meg. When he died, I asked that no one call me that anymore. It was personal to me, kind of like the last little thing I had of him."

John thought of the way Winslow insisted on calling her Meg. He was wondering why she had guarded this part of herself from the man she was about to marry. Or had she told him all this and he found it immaterial? Yeah, he was that kind of man. *And remember,* his subconscious whispered, *no matter this or anything else, she was about to marry him anyway.*

"Mom was different then," Megan continued. "She's still lovely to look at, but back then, she wasn't scared all the time, she wasn't aggressive or pushy. I guess because she relied on Dad to take care of her. Mom is a big believer in the notion that a woman is defined by a man. In her mind—and in fairness, her experience—a man is the one who takes care of the basics in life, the woman adds the color. He provides the foundation, she the substructure. He's the cake, she's the frosting."

John thought about Betsy, something he hadn't done in more than passing for a long while, something he didn't want to do now. He pushed all thoughts of her from his head and concentrated on what Megan was saying.

"After Dad died, everything at our house changed," she continued. "The money everyone thought we had wasn't there. Mom was reluctant to change our life-style so she ate up what we did have in a very short time, leaving us nothing but his pension—he was a lot older than she was. Our house began to fall apart around us and we had no money to fix it. The neighborhood deteriorated and we couldn't afford to move. I worked my way through school and Mom kept her eyes open for my ticket back to the life she thought was my birthright."

"And along came Robert Winslow."

Megan nodded. "We were at a fund-raiser. By chance, my mom was there, too. She saw Robert paying attention to me. By the next day, I swear, that woman knew everything there was to know about him. I still don't know how she did it. By the end of the month, she'd managed to throw us together half a dozen times, and things just took off from there."

John, who usually avoided these kinds of excruciatingly intimate discussions like a mouse avoids a trap, found himself musing aloud, "Which still doesn't explain why you fell in love with him."

"Maybe I didn't," she whispered. "Maybe I agreed to marry him because it was expected, because my mother wanted it so badly, because I didn't have the guts to concentrate on what it was *I* needed, maybe even because I didn't feel I deserved anyone better."

He nodded. He believed she was trying to understand her mistakes and learn from them, but he also believed it was hard for a horse to change color. She'd let herself get swept along with Winslow up to and including the "I do" in the wedding ceremony. He suspected that somewhere deep inside she was more like her mother than she knew, which meant she was a danger to…well, face it, to him as well as to herself.

Out of the blue, she changed course one hundred and eighty degrees and said, "Tell me about your ex-wife."

He had no intention of plunging into his own miserable past. He held up both hands and said, "Oh, no, you don't."

"No, I don't what?"

"I am not going to talk about Betsy."

She smiled. "So, that was her name. Betsy. Was she pretty?"

"Yes."

Now she bit her lip and her expression changed from playful to thoughtful. "What happened, John?"

"You mean, why did we get divorced? Easy. I thought marriage meant one thing and she thought it meant another. Now, please, I really don't want to talk about Betsy." He glanced at his watch again and added, "Look at the time."

She shook her head as she stretched luxuriously like a contented cat. When she stood, her clothes clung to her body, outlining every incredible curve. He looked away as he got to his feet.

"Okay, you're off the hook...for now," she added as she leaned down and patted Lily's head. Then she straightened and smiled at him. "I'll get all the gory details out of you sooner or later."

He changed the subject. "We're leaving here a little early tomorrow morning. I've finally thought of what you can do on the boat to repay me for trespassing into my inner sanctum."

"I trust it's something hideous."

"Are you afraid of heights?"

"Should I be?"

He grinned.

She gazed up at him. Her eyes were enormous under her yellow cap of hair, her face a pale oval punctuated by the dimples. She said, "John, are you really going to hire someone else to be captain?"

"I really am," he said.

She bit at her lip.

"Hey, maybe the new guy won't be such a sourpuss. Maybe he'll like kids."

"I hope so," she said, smiling.

He nodded, thoroughly alarmed to discover that what he hoped was that the interview would be so awful there would be no way on earth he could justify hiring this new guy.

This discovery shook him down to his feet.

She changed direction again when she said, "I'm sorry about today. I didn't mean to take advantage of you."

"No need to be sarcastic," he told her.

Grinning, she held out her hand. "Business associates?"

He shook her hand, exerting every ounce of self-control

he possessed not to pull her into his arms and finish what they'd started earlier that day. Oh, wouldn't she love that!

"I'll see you in the morning," she said. Before he knew it, she'd slipped on her coat, grabbed an umbrella and closed the sliding-glass door behind her.

He walked to the glass and stared out into the night, which was temporarily illuminated when Megan set off the motion sensor. All he could see of her was a red umbrella and slender legs. He turned his back.

Distance...that's what he needed, distance. He'd been doing fine less than a week ago before she'd bullied her way into his life. Tomorrow, if the captain's credentials were decent, he'd hire him on the spot. Megan had proven she was more than capable of handling the social aspects on the *Ruby Rose,* so he'd take that ad out of the paper and be blessedly free of phone calls.

That's what he'd do! He had a room down the hall that was half paneled, a piece of the rock wall to mend when the rain let up, an addition he was planning that would include a lap pool and spa. Summer was coming—there was the road to gravel and a garden to think about. Hell, there were literally dozens of things he needed to accomplish right here at this house. He was through with boats and hordes of people.

He looked at the model of the bronze tugboat which occupied a far corner. It was a model of the *Abaguzi,* the first tug he'd bought after maritime school, the beginning of what Betsy had called his fleet, a fleet she'd managed to destroy. He'd sold her years ago—the tug, not Betsy—but for just a second, he wondered what had become of the *Abaguzi.*

"Come on, Lily," he called as he flicked off the last light. She shuffled down the hall ahead of him.

Bright and early the next morning, Megan discovered the "chore" John had designed to pay her back for yesterday's so-called transgression. Perched on a canvas seat swinging from the top of a flag mast, she chanced a look down. What she saw made her head swim and her stomach lurch.

The deck was twenty feet below, but as it was attached to the top deck of the stern-wheeler, the water was another thirty feet past that. John stood at the base of the mast, ropes held tight—she hoped—her life in his hands. She had no idea how he had managed to talk her into letting him hike her up this spindly little mast to fix the flag pulley at the top. What did she care if the *Ruby Rose* couldn't fly a flag?

"How's it going?" he yelled.

"You just hold on to me," she called. "Remember, I'm heavier than I look!"

With his efforts, the canvas bosun chair inched up the mast until she saw the broken fitting. It took her a few minutes to unscrew the old and install the new, then another moment to feed a line through the shiny new pulley and drop the ends down to the deck. All this had to be accomplished with one hand and her chin because there was no way she was going to release her one-handed stranglehold of the mast.

She looked down between her knees again. "Okay, I'm done," she called. As the slow process of letting her down the mast began, she took a brave look around the gray deck, from the bow to the stern paddle, the wheelhouse, the line of plastic chairs against the metal rail, the lifeboat, the stairwells. It all looked so tidy from above, like such an orderly world.

Five feet up, John reached up and caught her, swinging her down to the deck in one fluid movement that started her stomach fluttering again. "That wasn't so bad, was it?"

"Not for you. I, however, am swearing off heights."

It wasn't yet seven o'clock and he hadn't put on his

captain's uniform. She liked him in jeans and a sweatshirt, she liked the grin that reminded her of a boy, she liked the way his eyes twinkled like sunlight on the water. "Now we're even," he said.

"Trust me, I will endeavor never to 'owe you one' again," she told him as she stepped out of the harness.

He folded the gear away with sure movements. "That's been needing done for a long time but I can't heft Dan and he can't heft me. Cook plain out refused, no deckhand would agree, and neither one of us could picture Mrs. Colpepper up there." He shuddered a little.

"Now you tell me," she said.

"I was afraid to tell you beforehand. Thanks, Megan. I'll finish tying this off and we'll fly Old Glory this morning."

She held her stomach with one hand and nodded, glad she'd been of help, determined to never be needed in that way again.

"I told Danny you'd go down and help him patch that deck," he added.

"Me?"

"Part of the job," he added.

"Great," Megan said. So far, aside from her regular duties, she'd painted inside trim, mopped the galley floor, changed two dozen light bulbs and been yarded up a flagpole. She'd loved every minute of it. Besides, she had a call to make, one she didn't want John to know anything about.

Between the birthday party for a twenty-one-year-old woman and the senior citizen tour, Megan noted the arrival of a man in his mid-thirties. Short, solid, fair-skinned and blond, features blunt and bland, he was the exact opposite of John Vermont. She watched as John greeted him on the main deck and they climbed the stairs to the wheelhouse.

Was this the man who had called about the position of captain?

Thirty minutes later, just as the first of the elderly passengers began coming aboard, some in wheelchairs, some with walkers, some with more pep than Megan felt, the stranger left. By the way he stood on the dock and stared at the stern-wheeler, it was obvious to Megan that he was considering this job.

Ignoring the hollow feeling inside, Megan helped a woman with hair as white as snowdrops onto an interior bench as the engines revved up for the impending excursion. She was dying of curiosity, but her job demanded that she stay with these folks and entertain them for the one-hour-and-forty-five-minute harbor cruise.

She pointed out bridges and grain barges, the college campus and the boatyard. She fetched coffee and juice, made a few jokes with Tyler Ponick, the cook who was himself revving up for the impending wedding dinner by heaping morsels of pineapple, melon, strawberries and grapes onto huge platters while the galley was filled with the aroma of herb-rubbed roast beef.

Finally, Danny helped her see their passengers safely off the ship, and then the two of them began setting up for the double wedding, which was slated to begin in less than an hour. Already, the two brides, along with two nervous mothers, were downstairs primping and fluffing. Two fathers paced the main deck and found fault with almost everything Megan did. Danny winked at her as though to tell her not to let it get to her, but she was glad when he enlisted the aid of the fathers and finished placing the awnings and flowers where *they* wanted them, relieving her to see if the women were any easier to get along with.

They weren't. Megan did everything they asked, a smile stapled in place, but she was glad when one of the brides dismissed her.

She made a quick trip to her cabin to change into the

navy dress and the dreaded heels, and to pencil the wedding parties' names into John's book. Seeing as she'd yet to have a moment to make her phone call, she took the opportunity to sit down and dial Robert's office.

She got through his secretary without any trouble though she'd bet money that the woman was now listening in on another line. She'd been at the flubbed wedding, too.

Robert's hello was brusque. "What is it, Meg?"

She didn't allow his purposeful use of her father's nickname make her angry. She said, "I'll be frank. I just want to ask you to leave John Vermont alone."

He laughed without humor. "Did he ask you to call?"

"No. Of course not—"

"Because you can tell him I'll have his sorry tail in court. I've got lawyers working on it right this minute."

"What happened is between you and me," she said, straining to remain calm. "It has nothing to do with him."

"You tell him that if he wants to apologize, he can come down here and do it himself, not send a woman."

The anger won. "You are such a conceited idiot, Robert Winslow. You can't even imagine me making a call of my own volition, can you?"

"You need a man, Meg," he said. "If it's not me, then it'll be someone like that sailor friend of yours. How long have you known him? Did you meet before the wedding, is that what this is all about?"

Refusing to rise to the bait, she said simply, "This is about you cutting your losses and not making a fool out of yourself by suing a man who had nothing to do with anything," she said.

"Like hell," he said, then he hung up on her.

Megan sat for some time in her chair trying to figure out if this ill-conceived plan of appealing to the better side of a man who apparently didn't have a better side had actually made things worse. At last, using the attached head, she splashed cold water on her face and took a few steadying breaths, then she went back to work, putting the call behind her.

The band was setting up amplifiers, the buffet was in final preparations, the cake had been delivered on time, and the engines were starting up for the trip downriver. It had only been two days and yet all of this was becoming routine.

What shocked her most was that in spite of the long hours and the sometimes rude people, she was enjoying herself in a way she hadn't since college. This work was so immediate. Things happened. When they were over, it was off to the next event. Gratification was swift.

And there was John, too, of course. She enjoyed seeing him off and on during the day, enjoyed his wicked wit, the verbal sparring, even the quiet moments he seemed so afraid of. And, of course, lingering like the taste of fine wine was the depth of passion she'd felt in his kiss. For an instant she imagined making love to him, having all that power and emotion possessing her. She took a couple of shallow breaths… It would never happen.

Even if he wanted it, which he obviously didn't, it was all too much, too soon. Once before, she had rushed headlong into a relationship; she was determined not to do it again. Not this time, not with this man.

Danny found her lingering at the bow on the lower deck, up near the anchor windlass, looking out at the water side of the harbor.

"Hey, beautiful," Danny said.

She smiled at his greeting. "Hi."

"The masses are beginning to gather on the dock," he said teasingly, referring to the wedding guests.

She glanced at her watch. It was almost time to board everyone.

Danny had green eyes the color of grass, sandy hair, and a beguiling smile. Apparently, from what she'd heard around the boat, lots of women found his boyish charm very attractive. Megan couldn't help but compare him to John, which was probably unfair to the poor guy.

"We haven't had much of a chance to get to know each other, have we?" he asked, cranking the handle on the windlass as though to tighten the anchor chain. Since they were docked and the anchor was already tight against the hull, she assumed this effort originated from nerves or an attempt to impress her with his muscles. Men were so transparent.

"No," she agreed.

"Maybe some night after work we can go out for a drink or dinner or…something."

He wasn't nervous… She had a fair idea what the "something" might be. She said, "Well, as I ride to and from work with John, we'd have to include him, too."

He nodded knowingly. "I thought you two might be eyeing each other."

"No, it's not like that," she said with half a smile. Hoping to change the subject, she added, "What are you doing?"

He gave the handle one last tug and shrugged. "Adjusting the brake on this thing." He stared right at her as though watching for her reaction. "It sounds like you haven't heard about Norm Richardson."

She blinked her eyes a couple of times. "Is that the name of the man John interviewed today?"

"One and the same. I met him—he seems nice enough. John is obviously relieved to have found him. I know how he hates this job. Now, about you and me…"

"And the dozens of your other admiring fans?" she quipped, though her heart suddenly felt overwhelmingly empty. *John was leaving the stern-wheeler….*

"Rumors," Danny said with a smile. "Just rumors."

As John struggled through the vows, his eyes kept finding Megan's and then he'd lose his place and have to struggle some more. At last, somehow, he switched into remote gear, his memory took over and the words fairly tumbled out. This was the way it had been at the beginning, before he'd taken the hiatus and gotten out of practice. Long before the day Megan had stepped aboard his boat.

He was doing the right thing. Every sensibility he possessed told him that hiring Norm Richardson was good, that it was high time he got away from this. And then his eyes met hers again and he felt rotten and he didn't even know why.

After the ceremony, she came up to him. "The flag looks great," she said.

Ignoring how good it felt to have her stand next to him, he looked above them at the stars and stripes snapping in the damp breeze. The rain had let up a little, thank goodness, though dark clouds hovered over the mountain peaks off to the east. He said, "Thanks to you."

She cleared her throat. "I hear you hired a new captain."

This brought his gaze back to her face. "He starts a week from Monday. You'll like him."

"Does he like kids?"

"I'm sure he adores them. He may be divorced but he says he has three of his own."

"Is that what it takes?" she mused, clasping the railing and gazing out at the river. "Does it take having kids to like them?"

"I don't know," he said. "For some people, I guess that's what it takes."

"For you?" she asked.

"I don't know," he repeated, unsure what her point was.

She smiled brightly. "I do," she said with conviction.

Still confused about what this talk of children was about he said, "You do?"

"Yep." She directed her gaze at him and added, "Truth of the matter is that you like kids right now."

"Is that right?"

"That's right. You really didn't mind them up in your wheelhouse—as a matter of fact, you liked it."

Amused, he repeated himself. "Is that right?"

"Yep. Of course, you'd rather swim through shark-infested water than admit it, but it's true."

He leaned against the rail and studied her face, which he realized with a shot of alarm was becoming very familiar. He told himself he had no desire to kiss her again, to hold her, to stroke her hair, to hear her sigh. Finally he said, "And how did you reach this startling conclusion, one, I might add, that I have never reached myself?"

"I watched you," she said unabashedly. "I watched you help them each toot your horn. I watched the way you watched them as they poked into all the corners, the gentle way you kept a hand on the rambunctious boy's shoulder, the soft way you tousled the little girl's head as she left."

"You do a lot of watching," he said. He still wasn't sure what she was getting at but she had such an endearing way of pursing her lips and then nibbling on them that he stared at her, transfixed. All he wanted was for her to continue talking. That she was talking nonsense was irrelevant.

"I know I do. I'm a watcher. So are you." She looked down at her feet and paused so long he understood that she was finished. Finished with what, however?

"Not that this isn't fascinating," he said, "but what exactly is your point?"

"I guess what I'm trying to say is that maybe you don't know yourself as well as you think you do."

"And what exactly does that mean?"

Straightening her shoulders as though she expected a blow, she said, "Do you really want to leave this vessel?"

Her question startled him. He said, "Of course I do! What kind of question is that?"

"I think you're kidding yourself," she said bluntly. "And I think you have everyone around here so buffaloed that they wouldn't tell you the truth on a bet."

"But you would?"

"Why not?"

"I see," he snapped angrily. "You've known me all of four days but you know my motives and secret desires better than I know them."

"You're upset," she mumbled.

"No, not upset, just confused. Correct me if I'm wrong, but aren't *you* the one who came within a gnat's breath of marrying an A-1 jerk? And aren't *you* the woman who confessed she got so caught up in her mother's dreams that she lost sight of her own? That was you, wasn't it?"

Megan's eyes narrowed.

"And now *you're* standing here telling *me* I don't know *my* mind? What kind of rot is that?"

"You're upset," she repeated.

"Yeah," he finally agreed. "I guess you're right, I guess I'm upset. Yesterday I wanted you to kiss me when I didn't even know it and today I'm hell-bent on leaving a boat I don't really want to leave. What would I do if I didn't have you to let me know what I really want?"

"You're mad because I'm telling you something you know is true in your heart of hearts."

"I don't think you have the slightest idea what's true in my heart of hearts."

"Then I'm sorry," she said softly and, shaking her head, walked away from him across the deck, down the stairs to the reception below.

John slammed his fist against the railing, swore under his breath and, cradling his throbbing hand, made his way to the sanctuary of the wheelhouse. Thank goodness he'd hired Norm Richardson.

Chapter Seven

They drove home in a silence so loud it screamed in Megan's ears. She *wasn't* going to talk first. Period. What was going on in his brain? Was he getting ready to fire her and kick her out of the guest house? If so, she was sure glad she hadn't yet invested any money in deck shoes!

As they turned into his driveway, he broke the silence. "If you want a ride in the morning, I'm planning on leaving at the usual time," he said without looking at her.

"Maybe I'll drive myself tomorrow," she said on impulse.

"Fine." He stopped the truck and switched off the lights but left the engine running and they sat side by side in the dark until, at last, he cleared his throat. "Megan, I've been thinking. We still have almost two weeks to go."

He meant it was twelve days until the new captain took over. She said, "I know."

"I don't want to spend it like this."

The beginning of a thaw? She could meet him halfway. She said, "Neither do I."

"I'm not saying that I agree with what you said earlier

about my not knowing what I want. I have always known what I want.''

Now was not the time to argue this point. Besides, he was right, what did she know about him? ''Okay,'' she said, chancing a glance in his direction. The dark hid his features, but she could tell he was looking at her.

''You have no idea how many years I've spent on boats or how much I hate getting mixed up in weddings I don't believe in or the horror of getting involved in embarrassing—''

''Scenes,'' she said, interrupting.

His laugh was shallow, but it broke a little of the tension. After another lengthy pause, he added, ''I think I'll go back down to the River Rat for dinner.''

''Sure,'' she said, unreasonably disappointed he didn't invite her to come with him. She'd seen the small restaurant on the side of the road, hanging out over the river like an uprooted tree, and it had seemed quaint and inviting. Obviously he wanted to reestablish his independence from her. Fine, if that's the way he wanted it—it wasn't as if they were involved with each other or anything. She could spend the evening tackling more of those wedding gifts in her mother's spare bedroom.

She opened her door and got out of the truck. The interior light had come on and she turned to find him staring at her.

Taking a deep breath, she said, ''If you want me to leave the boat or leave your guest house—''

''No,'' he interrupted. ''No, that's not what I want.''

''What do you want?''

Her question seemed to perplex him. Finally he said, ''I want you to continue doing what you do on the boat. You're a natural. I want you to be helpful to Norm when he shows up.''

''And until then?'' She knew she was pushing him, but she needed to get things straight.

"Everything pretty much the way it was," he said.

"With the exception of my stepping over the 'business only' line you drew in the sand."

"Yes," he said, without blinking.

"I see. Well, business as usual, nothing more, nothing less. I might as well catch a ride with you in the morning."

"Sure," he said.

She closed the door. His headlights swept the wet yard as he backed away from the house and turned around. She stood there in the icy drizzle and watched as his red tail-lights disappeared down the drive.

To some extent, John got his wish; things returned to more or less the way they'd been before Megan had had the audacity to suggest to him that he didn't know his own mind. She cooked dinner and he washed dishes. They both complained about the rain just like everyone else in Oregon did. They still occasionally sat in front of the fire at night. But the depth of their time alone changed in subtle ways until it was like an oil slick, glossy but right on the surface with no depth. Megan was startled to discover how much she missed what had so quickly been growing between them.

The exceptions came during wedding ceremonies, especially those in the afternoon. John would recite words of love and tenderness he professed not to believe, but which his delivery made profound. More often than not, his eyes would find hers as he spoke, and more often than not, she couldn't bring herself to look away. At those times, it seemed like the words were personal, words of a lover, a caress sent on the breeze, and she would recall the day he'd held her and kissed her as though there was no tomorrow.

It had all been going too quickly. And now it was dead in the water.

Two weeks after she'd shoved Robert overboard, she

found tears in her eyes during a ceremony—not an unusual occurrence for her except that these tears felt different. It wasn't until John pronounced the couple he was marrying husband and wife that she finally understood in what way her tears differed from the buckets she'd shed before; the conclusion made her heart ache.

These tears were for John, not for Robert. *How fickle is it,* she quizzed herself, *that a measly two weeks after dunking one man you can cry over another? What in the world is wrong with you?*

For the first time since John had told her he'd hired a replacement, she was glad. The past few days had proved they could share the property with no difficulty—it was on the boat that intimacy seemed to snare them both when they weren't looking, and it only went to figure that if he wasn't here, the wrenching moments during other people's weddings wouldn't happen.

Thank goodness he'd hired Norm Richardson!

Monday morning, John awoke early. He had his teeth brushed and the coffee machine switched on before he realized he didn't need to get up at the crack of dawn—that was Richardson's job now.

Well, he couldn't go back to bed, that wasn't his style. He took his shower and dressed in jeans and a red sweatshirt from his alma mater. The coffee was ready by then, and on impulse, he poured a second mug and put it on a tray to take to Megan. At the last second he remembered she liked sugar in her coffee, so he added the sugar bowl to the tray and, dodging Lily's attentions, made for the glass door.

Perhaps in honor of his getting his life back on track, the relentless rain was gone that morning. He could see the mountains off to the northeast and they fairly glowed, as white and pure as a virgin's wedding gown. Tulips had sprouted between the rhododendron bushes, making an irregular bank of pink blossoms and glossy green leaves that beautifully offset the rock wall. He set the tray down on the wall. Below him, in a river swollen by the rain, bobbed his little skiff, which was buttoned up with a canvas cover. The sluggish way she moved warned him she'd taken on water despite the cover and he made a mental note to go down later and bail her out.

Megan emerged from the guest house before he could find the courage to knock. Sometime over the weekend she'd bought herself some deck shoes and she wore them now with jeans and the red blazer. He thought she looked wonderful. She carried a paper sack in one hand.

"Coffee?" he called.

She smiled. Those smiles were few and far between lately, and the brilliance of this one put the sun to shame. His heart pounded as she approached and once again he told himself how smart he was to have hired Norm.

Okay, he'd been angry with her for questioning his motives when it came to leaving the stern-wheeler. That on the heels of the whole who-kissed-who fiasco had cautioned him to keep his distance. She'd responded by keeping hers, too. Oh, once in a while they would look at each other during a ceremony, that was to be expected. Did she realize she was still crying over her own botched wedding, that tears glistened in her eyes, catching the sun, making them shine like diamonds?

He thought it was safe to say she was still working out her feelings for that louse. So he'd protected himself…only smart thing to do.

However, enough was enough. It was hard to maintain this stream of heady indignation, and besides, they would be spending hours apart from now on. He could risk a little coziness.

"I'm running late," she said, glancing at her watch.

"You have time for coffee," he said.

She shook her golden head. "I can't be late for my first

day with the new boss." She flashed him another mind-boggling smile and added, "See you tonight. Have a good day."

"You, too." She'd taken a few steps away when he called, "Hey, what's in the sack?"

She stopped, twirled around and faced him. "Disposable cameras," she said with a bewitching grin.

Though he had never admitted it to her, he'd thought the camera idea was a good one, and he'd often wondered why she'd let the ball drop. Now, as soon as he was off the ship, she was forging ahead. Was she planning on taking over now that he was gone? A smile tilted his lips as he thought to himself that Norm Richardson better stay on his toes!

John nailed and bailed and painted his way through the day. Taking off his sweatshirt, he ate a solitary lunch on the rock wall, determined to soak up as much of the sun as possible. The heat felt great on his back but already he could see clouds gathering in the distance and he feared more rain was imminent.

He tried not to think about the *Ruby Rose* or Megan or even Foggy Dew who had to be close to giving birth. He tried not to wonder what Richardson was like as a captain, how Megan would compare them, in what ways she might prefer Norm's approach over his. He knew for a fact that there was a third grade class doing a tour today. No doubt Megan would take every last kid up to the wheelhouse and inflict them on Norm, and no doubt, Norm would rise to the occasion and be charming and good natured about it.

His thoughts returned to the cat. As he wrapped new wire around a post on his northeast property corner, he worried that she might choose some totally unsafe spot to have her family—he would have to warn Megan to put a box in his cabin for the cat. Damn! It wasn't his cabin anymore. How did you ask a man you just hired to share his quarters with a pregnant cat? No matter, he'd think of something. There was a small room down between the galley and the engine room. That was it, that was where she could be locked until the big event was over.

Would he miss the birth? It seemed likely. Maybe he should bring her to the house and lock her in the garage, safely away from Lily. Somehow, though, it didn't seem right to take the cat away from what seemed to be the only home she'd ever known right on the eve of this big event.

He would leave her on the boat and caution Megan to look out for her.

Lily woofed at the ghostly passing of a blue heron as it glided to a stop in the marshy meadow next door. John took a breather to admire the bird. A couple of black-and-white cows that had called the meadow home for years mooed at him. He put the pliers in his work belt and wiped the sweat off his forehead with a blue kerchief. It felt good to be right where he was, doing exactly what he was doing.

Megan arrived home an hour before the sun was slated to disappear. John was just in the process of starting the gas grill on the rock patio. He'd stopped work early, taken a shower, marinated some chicken in a sauce that came in a package—just add oil and water—and tossed a salad. He thought her first day of work on the stern-wheeler alone deserved some sort of recognition.

She wasn't alone, you idiot. Norm was there and Danny. However, Danny, with his track record with pretty women, was someone he preferred not to think about.

In the moment before she saw him, her expression was thoughtful. Her somber expression lightened perceptibly when she caught him staring. As she veered toward the barbecue, he found all his senses heightened just because she was moving closer to him. She must realize the seductive way she walked, the sway to her hips, the habit she had of looking down at the ground and then ahead without raising her head all the way.

Controlling his emotions wasn't as easy as it used to be.

"You're cooking?"

"First barbecue of the season," he said.

She looked up at the clouds. "You don't think you're pushing it?"

"Probably. But I live life on the edge."

The new smile was more genuine. "I see."

"Besides, I thought you could use a break and this is the only kind of cooking I know how to do. It'll take the chicken an hour or so to cook, plenty of time for you to take a hot bath or…whatever."

He stopped babbling when a vision of her nude, stepping into the bathtub, steam rising up her long legs, stole his breath. He blinked a couple of times and added, "Or I could just pour you a glass of wine."

"I like the sound of that bath," she said softly.

"How did the cameras go over?"

Her smile had a kind of wistful quality to it as she said, "All right. How did you like staying home?"

"Fine," he said heartily. "And how was your first day with Norm?"

"Great," she told him and, turning, entered the guest house.

Great? That's not what he wanted to hear. He wanted details, damn it! Well, he'd ask her again after they ate. Sullen, without having the vaguest idea why, he went to get the chicken out of the refrigerator.

She returned as he set a small table under a sizable awning. It was getting cold, but he'd also dragged out an old propane heater that kept the sheltered area toasty warm.

The table was covered with a white cloth and pink napkins he'd found in the sideboard but didn't recall buying. They were probably some Betsy had forgotten to take with her. He'd picked a couple of the pale pink tulips and shoved them into a wineglass. They sat in the middle of the table now, their heavy heads drooping.

"How pretty," she said.

Looking at her, he could only agree. By chance, she'd chosen a filmy pink dress that matched the glow in her cheeks. Her hair was still damp, curling at her temples. The table, which had looked kind of wan, came to life the moment she sat in her chair.

"There's a couple of things I wanted to talk to you about," he said.

"Okay."

"Well, I've been thinking about Foggy Dew. I'm concerned she might have her kittens in an unsafe place and now that my cabin is more or less off limits—"

She interrupted him. "The same thought crossed my mind, so earlier today, I put a box in my office, in a dark corner of the closet with a couple of old towels in it. She seems quite content there."

"Oh."

"Is that all right?"

"What? Oh, sure, that's great."

"What else?" she asked as he poured the wine.

"Nothing that won't wait until after dinner," he said, retreating to the barbecue.

They ate the salad and the chicken, drank a glass of wine, then sat back as the rain began to fall. She looked toward the river, seemingly content. He couldn't get out of his mind the thoughtful expression she'd worn earlier, and a niggling suspicion that everything wasn't right on the stern-wheeler returned to him. He decided to try it again. "Megan, how did it go today?"

"On the boat?"

Where else he silently screamed, but said, "Yes, on the boat."

She shrugged. "Like I said, everything went fine."

"That says nothing."

"That says it all," she insisted.

He swallowed his impatience and tried another tack. "So, do you like Norm?"

"He seems to know what he's doing," she said.

"He's very qualified," he said.

Megan nodded.

"How about the class trip?"

"Couldn't have been smoother." She leaned forward a little and smiled like a cat who had just cornered a plump canary. "What's wrong, do you miss the boat?"

He laughed. "Hardly. What about Norm? Did he like having the kids in the wheelhouse?"

"He seemed to."

"Did he let them toot the horn?"

She took a deep breath. "John, at the risk of offending you, may I be blunt?"

He wanted to tell her no, she could not risk offending him. They were just getting over the last time, couldn't she see that? Couldn't she just answer his questions and leave well enough alone? He said, "Go ahead."

"You don't want anything to do with the stern-wheeler past an owner's desire that it pay its way, right?"

"It never pays its way," he mumbled. "My tax man loves the old tub. Why do you think I keep it?"

"Answer me," she said calmly.

"Okay," he said. "You're right."

"So, don't question me about it. It makes me feel like a spy. If you want to know how Norm liked the kids, ask Norm. I'm trying very hard not to step on your toes, but if you keep sticking your foot out in front of me—"

"I get your point," he interrupted.

Lowering her eyes and her voice, she added, "And you don't have to entertain me just to pump me for information—"

"Is that what you think I'm doing?" he snapped.

Her eyes suddenly seemed moist. "Aren't you?"

"No," he said, practically strangling. This whole conversation was perilously close to escalating into a...a scene.

"Then what?"

"I don't know," he said, throwing up his hands.

Looking straight at him, she said, "I thought you knew everything." She stood abruptly. "Thanks for dinner, it was delicious. Since you cooked, I'll wash."

John, speechless, sat there while she cleared the table. Then he called Lily and, heedless of the downpour, took off along the bluff for a brisk walk to clear his head.

"Punctuality, Miss Morison, as I have said a dozen times, is a trait I value in my crew."

Megan looked at Norm Richardson's round face and internally sighed. She'd been late boarding passengers because Foggy Dew had finally started having her kittens. It seemed wrong to leave the little cat alone at such a time, but ultimately she had, ushering all the wedding guests on deck only five minutes behind schedule. During the proceedings, she'd used every opportunity to check on Foggy Dew's progress. Now, hours later, there were five little furry gray bodies in with their mom, all tucked safely away in the closet in a sturdy box, and Megan was in trouble.

For the past ten days, ever since Norm had come aboard, he had used this time at the end of the workday to point out any mistakes anyone made. Danny had been called to the carpet three times for flirting with guests. Tyler Ponick had taken heat over his coffee—it was too strong, and no, the captain didn't want decaf, he just wanted the cook to water down the real stuff. Three days before, Megan had caught it for being late for a wedding, even though she'd been down below, the hysterical bride clinging to her, so the ceremony hadn't even started.

And, oh, yes, there was the disposable camera issue...

"Richardson's a competent captain," Danny had said in

a private huff, "and I'd never complain to John, but the man is just too much like Agnes Colpepper for my taste."

Amen.

"What's your excuse?" Norm asked in his patronizing tone.

"I have no excuse," Megan said. She wasn't about to tell him about Foggy Dew. Somehow, by some miracle, the cat had escaped Norm's attention. It was hard to imagine he would be enchanted with the idea of running a ship with kittens aboard. She'd have to figure out some way to hide the little family until everyone was old enough to go to new homes.

Or you could tell John...

This thought had been fluttering around in her brain since the first day Norm had taken over command of the *Ruby Rose.* How she had yearned that first night to tell John what a prig Norm was, how he robbed the ship of fun, how he patronized everyone, how the kids didn't even like him.

And then he'd started asking questions and she'd bristled and made her holier-than-thou declaration that she would not talk about Norm behind his back. John had stopped asking, though he still continued to cook and she was stuck with her own rules—that and enough barbecued meat to feed a hungry hoard of ranch hands.

Besides, if John really hated being aboard the *Ruby Rose,* she wasn't going to be the one to rob him of his peace of mind. She knew that he hadn't actually hired anyone to take over for him until the day after he'd kissed her and they'd become so self-conscious about it. Some part of her felt as though she was the straw that broke the poor old camel's back and she felt rotten about it.

Well, apparently, Norm knew how to skipper the boat and if that was all John wanted, then so be it. If she didn't like the situation, the solution was easy—she could get another job.

And leave John in the lurch?

"Then see it doesn't happen again," Norm said stiffly. Consulting his clipboard, he added, "Three weddings tomorrow."

Megan nodded. She already knew this. For days she'd stood by while he delivered the wedding vows in a monotone, his brass buttons shining brighter than his eyes, his fancy braid-covered hat the liveliest thing about him. The man was no John Vermont!

But then, who was?

"—then there's smooth sailing until the dinner-dance next week."

The dinner-dance… For weeks she'd been making plans to assure its success while trying to think of a way out of actually attending it.

"How is everything going concerning this party?" Norm quizzed.

She said, "Fine." Period. She did not want him sticking his nose into the details. Once again, she thought of excuses for being absent on the big night, and once again, discarded them all. With John, she may have been able to cajole a replacement, but with Norm?

"Okay, then," he finished. "And remember, schedules are important for a tightly run ship."

"Aye, aye, sir," Megan muttered under her breath.

John expertly rowed the skiff next to the small dock. As he caught the line dangling from the cleat, Lily disobeyed his command to sit and launched herself out of the boat. She was halfway up the cliff before he had finished tying the skiff and had disappeared completely by the time he'd snapped on the canvas cover.

Picking up his fishing gear, he started the climb, pausing at the first plateau to look back at the river. It was running high this year due to all the rain, even his lazy inlet was more turbulent than it had been in the past.

He hadn't caught a fish. He hadn't even gotten a bite, but he didn't really care. Just being out on the water was joy enough; he didn't need to catch anything to have fun. 'Course, it would have been nice to barbecue Megan a fish he'd caught himself.

This thought made his gut restless and he started hiking again. Every time he tried to figure out why he felt so compelled to cook for Megan, he was left with a blank. An uneasy blank. He recalled the first time he'd met her and the involuntary instinct to protect her that had assailed him. That instinct had led to her becoming a fixture at his home.

The truth of the matter was that women in general and that woman in particular didn't need to be protected—quite the contrary. You'd think he'd learn.

Every night she came home full of praise for Norm Richardson, for whom John had unfairly taken a general dislike due solely to the fact that Norm seemed to be doing such a bang-up job. Now that was bad enough. That was just out-and-out dumb—he'd never been prone to feelings like these and he didn't appreciate them now. What made it worse was that night after night she told him everything on the stern-wheeler was hunky-dory but she never shared a single detail unless it was something about Foggy Dew, a passenger, or something she'd spied on the shore.

After the way she had overreacted to his asking a few harmless questions, he wasn't about to be the inquisitive one—would it kill her to volunteer information once in a while? Nothing spectacular, he wasn't looking for dirt. Truth was, he felt shut out and abandoned.

What in the world was *that* all about? The only thing he could think of was that Megan had been right. He hadn't wanted to leave the *Ruby Rose* after all. He'd made a mistake.

This thought was so outrageous that as he came across Lily panting at him from atop the rock wall, he ranted and raved at her, chastising her for jumping out of the boat instead of staying put the way she'd been told. Since it had all happened fifteen minutes before, he knew in his head that by now the Lab's memory of the event was hazy at best, but it felt good to raise his voice and shout. As she pretty much ignored him anyway, no harm was done.

He stopped when he heard a giggle. Megan was standing a few feet beyond the dog. He hadn't even seen her. Her eyes amused, she asked, "Catch anything?"

"Females," he sputtered. "Not a one of you does what you're told to do."

This only earned him another giggle.

"How many?"

Megan looked up from peeling a carrot into paper-thin strips and said, "Five. All of them are gray, like their mom. And they're so tiny, John." She watched his lips curve into a slow smile as his imagination furnished him a picture of his cat and her babies, and she found a big old knot forming at the base of her throat.

"What did Norm think of them?" he asked. He was sitting at the counter watching her cook. She'd stopped at the store on the way home and picked up pasta and vegetables and, without asking him what his dinner plans were, had just started making them something to eat that had nothing to do with a barbecue.

"Well—"

"I know," he interrupted. "You don't like to talk about Norm."

She began the same procedure on a zucchini, sparing him a quick glance as she did so. "No, normally I don't, but since it's your cat and your boat, I guess I should mention that Norm doesn't seem to know there's a cat aboard, let alone a whole family of them."

He was in the process of swiping a ribbon of carrot

when his hand paused and he looked up at her. "That has to be...awkward."

She didn't like the worry lines that had shown up on his forehead. She said, "Not really. I plan on keeping them all in my cabin. He never goes in there." She didn't add that he never went in because she kept it locked. As long as they were talking about men she could live without, she added, "What about Robert? Have you heard from him? Is he really going to sue you?"

John shrugged. "Given today's climate on lawsuits, I imagine he'll try to figure an angle."

"Aren't you worried about it?"

He seemed to consider this possibility as though it hadn't occurred to him before. Finally he said, "No. Should I be?"

"He's very powerful—"

"He's a jerk."

"A powerful jerk."

Again he shrugged. "If he sues me, I'll deal with it. You just stay out of it, okay? You have enough past with this bozo, you don't need this."

Bristling, she said, "Is that an order?"

This brought a smile to his lips. "No, that's a request. I'm a big boy, I can handle my own problems."

She nodded and hoped he never found out she'd called Robert on his behalf. As if it had done any good...

"Foggy Dew, a mom," John mused. "I'm sorry I missed it."

"I am, too," she said. "You'll have to come down and see them."

This simple statement seemed to make him shift in his seat. He finally said, "I don't know."

"Why?"

He shrugged his broad shoulders and fixed her with a blue stare. "I kind of told myself I'd take a real hands-off approach to the boat from now on."

Megan said, "Well, you wouldn't really be checking on the boat or Norm, would you? I mean, it's Foggy Dew you'd be coming to see."

She wondered if he had any idea how his eyes lit up when an idea pleased him. Did he know how much he missed the daily rigors of the stern-wheeler, or was she just imagining things? She looked at him fondly, acknowledging the warm spot she held in her heart for this contrary man who was so sure he knew every little detail about himself.

Adding garlic to a pat of butter, she sautéed the vegetables until they were limp. She could feel John staring at her. "You want to grate some of that Parmesan cheese?"

He got out the grater and the cheese while she tossed the vegetables with cooked fettucine and checked on the garlic bread.

Much to Megan's horror, John augmented his dinner with leftover barbecued ribs. When he caught her staring at him, he said, "What's wrong?"

"What is it with men and meat?"

He grinned. "I don't know. What is it with women and pasta?"

"We're a couple of sexists," she mused.

"Betsy liked pasta, too," he volunteered, which shocked Megan. He was talking about his ex-wife without even being prompted! She tried to look interested without looking too interested, and he elaborated.

"She wasn't as good a cook as you are but she could boil water and dump in noodles so we ate a lot of it. How did you learn to cook?"

Megan wanted to hear more about Betsy, not talk about herself, but what was conversation if not give and take? She said, "After Dad died and we ran out of money to pay the help, Mom started cooking for us. Her specialty was a microwaved baked potato smothered with canned creamed corn. She alternated this feast with burned bacon sandwiches. My survival instincts kicked in almost immediately so I bought a cookbook with money from my paper route and took over kitchen duty.''

"You had a paper route?"

"Best arm in the neighborhood," she said, flexing her muscles.

"Me, too. I grew up in Southern California, down where the summers are long and dry and hot, so I also had a lemonade stand.''

"Yard work?"

"Yep. Mowing lawns, clipping hedges.''

"I baby-sat.''

"I didn't.''

"Why am I not surprised? Were you an only child, too?"

"Not at first. My mother and little brother died in an auto crash when I was five. Dad raised me on his sailboat, the same one he still lives on down in Redondo Beach. He's a neat guy, you'd like him.''

"I'd like to meet him," she said.

He looked right into her eyes and smiled. For a second she felt as though her head was reeling; in fact, she felt very much as she had the day she was hoisted up that spindly mast. But this time she had both feet on the ground, she wasn't dangling fifty feet above the river.

"Betsy was an only child, too," he said, almost reluctantly. "A pampered only child. A little beauty queen as a kid, a Junior Miss Orange Juice or Orange County or something.'' He paused so long that Megan was sure the well had dried up when he added, "I don't know why she married me.''

Didn't he? Hadn't he ever looked in a mirror? Hadn't he ever seen his reflection as he strode across a deck or smiled at a child or fondled a dog's ears? Did he truly not understand what his voice could do, what his arms could do, what gentleness, what strength were in his hands, what suppressed passion trembled inside him? And had he never caught sight of himself in her eyes?

"I guess I'm still kidding myself," he said suddenly, dropping his fork. "Betsy married me because I was wealthy. When she discovered how much hard work and many long hours went into the acquisition of money, she occupied herself with diversions." He looked right into Megan's eyes and a bitter smile tilted his lips. "She made it with the golf pro at the country club she insisted we join. Can you imagine a bigger cliché? A golf pro, for heaven's sake. Then there was a race-car driver, a football player, and I believe a tennis champ."

How could any woman have the privilege of making love to John Vermont and throw it away for meaningless sex with other men? It boggled Megan's imagination.

"Betsy liked athletes," he added. "I was lucky to get a divorce, I know that now."

"But I bet it hurt at the time."

Again he met her gaze. "Damn right. I sold those tugs you saw that first day you came to work on the *Ruby Rose* so I could make a huge one-time payment to be rid of her. I kept the stern-wheeler because I'd just salvaged it and it was something Betsy had never stepped foot on, never derived a penny from, never tainted with her knowledge or presence. I suppose you think this sounds kind of warped."

"You forget you're talking to a woman who broke up with a man at the last second by shoving him off a boat," she said with a smile. "It doesn't sound warped at all. Actually, for me, the question isn't why Betsy married you, but why you married Betsy."

Sighing, he picked up his fork and tackled his food. Before any made it to his mouth, he abandoned the fork again. "I thought I loved her. She was the first woman who caught my eye. She...well, she needed me."

"You wanted to rescue her from herself," Megan said.

"Yes. She was half a woman and I thought I could make her whole, which makes me less than whole myself, doesn't it?"

"I don't know," Megan said.

"A whole man wants a whole woman. A man who needs to feel like a knight in shining armor wants a woman to cling to him. It's a symbiotic relationship."

"And that's what you felt like with her, a knight in shining armor?"

"For a while," he said, shaking his head. "That's why I don't trust marriage. People come at it from all sorts of weak places and strange angles."

"Don't I know it," she commiserated.

"I see it every day."

"But people can grow," she protested. "I imagine since you know all this about yourself, you're more careful now."

"You'd think," he said in such a way that Megan felt as though she'd been stabbed. Was he comparing her and Robert to him and Betsy? Wait. Worse—was he comparing him and Betsy to him and her? Was he trying to tell her that he was through with weak women set on snapping up strong men? Is that what he thought of her?

"For once, it's not raining. Let's leave the dishes and take a walk," he said suddenly, rising.

Megan folded her napkin. A walk seemed like a good idea.

Chapter Eight

The moon was full and hung in the sky like a giant glowing ball ready to drop to earth from its own sheer weight. There were stars, too, but they were faded by the moon, just hints of brilliance in the eternity above. The air was moist and cool and sent a chill through John's body.

He stopped at the top of the path and turned to Megan. "Are you warm enough?"

Megan finished buttoning her light coat and nodded. She looked enchanting in the silvery light. He said, "I know this path well enough to walk down to the river with my eyes shut, but it might be too dark for you..."

"Lead on," she said.

For safety's sake, he reached for her hand. It slipped so easily into his that it might have been custom fit. Lily darted off ahead of them and they began the descent to the river, the sound of rushing water growing louder with each step. Megan was right behind him, her breathing soft, her presence comforting and disturbing at the same time.

What had possessed him to ramble on and on about Betsy? It had happened without plan, as though he'd been waiting for years to share all the lurid details of his failed marriage with someone. At times, he'd been tempted to talk to Danny about Betsy but he never had; Danny was just too flighty. So, he'd never talked to a living soul... until Megan came along.

He thought about his dad and how vehemently he'd warned John about getting tangled up with Betsy. His old man had been right on about John's first wife. He'd said she was immature and selfish and needy, that her emptiness would swallow him whole, that he should run, not walk, away from this woman. John had known better, though. Ha!

They made it to the plateau within minutes. "This is a level spot above the river," he told her as they stood side by side, hands now separated and shoved into coat pockets. Lily could be heard off in the brush snuffling after the scent of some little woodland creature. The river was a gray ribbon below them, the trees on the far shore dark, lacy silhouettes against the lighter sky. For some reason the moon and stars always looked closer when viewed from this vantage point.

They sat on the grass, leaning back against an outcropping of rock, knees bent, the world before their eyes. For some time they were quiet and John found himself thinking of all the times he'd watched Megan walk away from him—off to work at the stern-wheeler, off to bed every night. Those were the most difficult times, when he had to remind himself that he wasn't about to get tied up with her, when he had to keep reminding himself why, when half the time, he couldn't think of a single reason and the remembered taste of her lips sent his head reeling.

"Thanks," she said, her voice almost a whisper as though she didn't want to trespass on his thoughts. Truth of the matter was, his thoughts were erratic and disturbing and he welcomed the interruption.

"Thanks for what?"

"For telling me about Betsy. For trusting me."

"You're welcome," he said, hoping she wouldn't bring it up again.

"Look at that moon. It looks like you could touch it, doesn't it? Have you ever in your life seen anything prettier?"

Staring at her face bathed in moon glow, he could honestly answer that question with a resounding yes. He had seen something more beautiful; he was looking at it right now. He made a soft sound of agreement as she rested her head on her knees, looking right at him—hell, right into him, maybe even right through him.

"John? Tell me about the dinner-dance."

For a second he was stymied as to what she was talking about. His thoughts had been in a whole different stratosphere. "You mean, the media party on the boat?"

"Yes."

"What do you want to know?"

After a pause that could only be labeled pregnant, she said, "I could hem and haw, but the bottom line is, I want to know if Robert Winslow is going to be there."

He couldn't help it, he didn't want her thinking about Robert, and he sure as hell didn't want the jerk's name mentioned on a night alight with magic. "You'd probably know the answer to that more than I would," he said.

Her head snapped up. "Are you implying—"

"I'm not implying anything," he said. "I only meant that I have no idea which individuals will attend. I know only what Colpepper wrote on that sheet of paper I believe you now have."

"The only names are those of the organizers, who I know, but I'll be damned if I'll call them. The whole lot of them were at my wedding. My almost wedding, that is. Anyway, this dinner-dance is the kind of social party we— he—always attends. He loves to hobnob with television and radio people. Publicity, you know."

John said, "I could pull strings with Norm. I could tell him he needs to hire outside help for that night."

"But you have a hands-off policy," she said.

"Rules are made to be broken," he said, admiring the curve of her cheek.

She was very quiet for a long time then she scooted down until she was lying on her back and gazing skyward, her hands folded across her stomach.

He scuttled down, too, lying on his side, his head propped on his hand. He was staring at the girl, not the moon. She gave no indication that she noticed him eating her alive with his eyes. She had to be aware of it though.

Of course she was aware of it…women always knew when they had a man coming and going. But if he knew he was being manipulated, couldn't he just go along with it for one night and let his senses take over? He wished he hadn't talked about Betsy. He wished he could get over the parallels in the two women. There were differences, too…he would concentrate on their differences.

She turned her face to his. "It was very kind, very sweet, of you to offer to bail me out of the party."

Her voice was softer than Betsy's. It never held that petulant tone that had let him know he was failing her, always failing her. He said, "That's the kind of guy I am."

A short, lilting laugh was followed by the words, "Let me finish. You don't need to talk to Norm. I can handle whatever Robert dishes out."

She was more independent, more competent, more self-assured in the ways that counted than Betsy ever dreamed of being. "I have no doubt of that," he said. "It's up to you. I was just reacting to the unease I could hear in your voice."

"I know you were. I wish I hadn't even mentioned it. Anyway, I'll bet you ten bucks he brings another woman with him and makes sure I know about it."

"Why would he do that?"

"To try to make me jealous."

"And will it?"

"No."

John suddenly noticed he'd reached over and touched her cheek. Good heavens, her skin was softer, her eyes more luminous, her mouth more tantalizing. As beautiful as Betsy had been, she couldn't hold a candle to this woman. Dropping his hand, he forgot about Betsy.

"I make you very nervous, don't I?" she asked.

"No," he said. "Yes."

"You're looking at me that way again," she said.

"I can't help myself."

"So, you admit it was your looking at me that led to all that fuss about your kissing me."

"I kissed you first with my eyes," he said softly, doing it again.

"The last time we kissed you said it was all my fault."

"I know," he whispered, lowering his head until their lips touched. Hers were as he recalled, softer than velvet, sweet and sensual, with an underlying current that aroused him immediately.

He pulled back for a moment, anxious to see what expression she wore. The gleam he could detect in her heavily shadowed face stole his breath. She put her palm against his cheek. When she ran her fingertips across his lips, he felt his heartbeat quadruple. Her own lips curled into a secret smile that seemed as fresh as spring buds and as old as the world.

"I refuse to take full credit for this," she whispered.

"I accept my share of the blame," he breathed, and proceeded to kiss her again.

This time there was no need to seek her approval or response. He brushed his lips across her eyelids, smoothed her hair away from her forehead and kissed the downy edge of her hairline. By the time he got to her lips again, he felt a startling heat growing in his loins. His hand slid hungrily down the curves of her body, pulling her hips against his. It had been so long since he'd been with a woman this way, but more than that, he'd been dying to be with *this* woman since the moment he'd first set eyes on her, dressed in white, standing at the altar about to marry the wrong man.

The river, the moon, even the damp chill of the earth on which they lay, were banished as he absorbed the very essence of Megan Ashley Morison. The smell of her hair. The satiny feel of her skin as his hand found her bare back. The small gasps she made as his kisses became deeper and his fingers moved beneath her waistband to touch the smooth, taut skin of her backside.

He was lost. He was lost and he didn't care.

Megan felt like a very small leaf being swept out to sea on a very large wave. The weight of John's body partially atop hers left her as breathless as his kisses. Their legs were intertwined and his hand was massaging her back. She could sense, in the one or two lucid moments she had between kisses, that he was quickly becoming so aroused that there would be no turning back. She'd never kissed a man with so much pent-up passion and it both excited and frightened her.

She had not meant for this to happen. That she had wanted it to happen was obvious from her ready response to his playful remarks, but wanting was not enough. This was a self-proclaimed marriage hater who had made it clear what he thought of her. If her emotions could bypass her common sense, his could do the same.

All this realization came and went in a flash, completely drowned out by the tide of sensations that assaulted her from every angle. She cupped his face in her hands and kissed him from forehead to nose to lips to ears, settling at last, with pleasure, on his lips. He held her so tight she felt almost faint.

"Oh, Meg," he whispered against her ear. "I could devour you."

Unbidden, swiftly, like a knife attack in a dark alley, Robert's image skittered across her brain. While it was gone in a flash, the impact was devastating. The world, and all the realities she had tried so hard to ignore, came crashing back into focus.

Gasping, she pulled herself away and sat. She could hear John's ragged breaths as he raised himself up beside her.

"What's wrong?" he asked, his voice husky and worried.

"N-nothing," she stammered.

"Nothing!"

She shook her head. "Really, it's nothing."

He was quiet for the longest minute Megan had ever endured, then he groaned. "I called you Meg," he said.

"John—"

"Damn!"

"It's okay," she said, straightening her rumpled clothes. "It's natural to shorten a person's name. I shouldn't be so hung up on it."

"Your father called you Meg," he said, his voice suddenly gentle as he caressed her ear.

"And so did Robert."

He dropped his hand. She said, "I'm sorry, John—"

"So I made you think of your ex-fiancé."

"No...no, of course not."

"Yes, I did."

She turned miserable eyes to his face and, reaching up, touched his cheek. "You're right, hearing my name shortened made me think of Robert, which was kind of like taking a dose of vinegar. It threw me, that's all."

He caught her hand and held it in the space between them. "I guess a man doesn't like to hear that a woman he's involved with is preoccupied with another man."

"It's not like that..."

"Isn't it? Your father called you Meg, but it wasn't he who popped into your thoughts, it was Winslow."

His eyes were dark pools in his face, reflecting little, telling even less. She knew this impression was due to the way his head was turned but it made her feel separated from him by more than the twelve inches between their noses.

"I don't know for sure what happened," she said truthfully. "One minute I was being swept away by you, and the next, Robert's face…well, it jolted me, that's all."

"You and me both," he said. His voice was flat—she had no idea what he was thinking and she was afraid to ask. She did not want it to be like this… She wanted to throw herself back into his arms and ask him to love all her doubts away, but her head felt like a puzzle box full of loose jagged pieces and it wasn't up to him to fit them together. That was her job.

He'd said he'd tried to save Betsy, he'd been her knight in shining armor. In many ways her own predicament with Robert was fueled by the same emotions gone awry. It hadn't worked for either of them, it never did. She would not allow them to fall into a pattern that had almost destroyed them both. She didn't want to hurt him; she didn't want to be hurt.

She ran her hand down his arm. "Maybe I need a little time to sort things through…" she began.

"Yeah, maybe you do," he said, standing abruptly and extending a hand to pull her to her feet. They regarded each other in the moonlight until at last he added, "Trouble is, we keep getting off track, Megan. It's my fault, I admit it. We have a perfectly fine arrangement that I keep messing with."

"John—"

"I mean, why fix something that isn't broken?"

"In other words, why change the status quo?"

"Exactly."

"Because people change," she said softly. "Nothing stays the same. *We've* changed."

"Not really," he said bluntly. "I think you are exactly who you've always been."

That was an insult on so many levels that her head throbbed from the sheer effort of trying to sort them out. She turned away and began marching back up the hill. She heard John call her name, but by then she was almost running. She was in the guest house before he had topped the hill.

He watched her leave the next morning through a corner of his bedroom window. Lily barked from the foot of his bed, reclaiming his attention.

"Get down from there," he told her as he tucked a flannel shirt into his well-worn jeans.

She reluctantly jumped to the floor, tail wagging, anticipating the morning walk she'd gotten used to since he'd quit going to work on the stern-wheeler.

He felt lousy this morning. Maybe he had the flu, he thought as he put on a coat and took off with the silly dog. He knew it wasn't really the flu, but he almost wished it was so he'd have something on which he could hang the gnawing feeling in the pit of his stomach. They walked a mile or two while he tried not to think about the night before, but the memory of Megan in his arms was so alive it pulsed through his blood.

After lunch, he stared at the phone.

He missed going to the damn boat. How in blazes had that ever happened?

Or was it the woman? Was it Megan? If it was her, then he needed to go chop firewood and get his mind on other things. She was the one who couldn't stand hearing the truth. She was the one who had walked away from him! And why? Because he didn't think she'd changed much?

She'd been as involved in their lovemaking as he'd

been, he was sure of it. A man knows when a woman is
faking things, and she hadn't been faking. And then he'd
uttered *Meg* and she'd changed in a blink, going from pas-
sionate to wary to a million miles away.

Had there been a wistful note in her voice when she'd
mentioned Robert's name? Good heavens, was it possible
the woman still harbored feelings for that man, feelings
that perhaps she herself was denying?

Face it—Megan Morison was confused. Once again
he'd avoided facing the cold, hard facts—beauty and
sweetness and that quirky streak of spirit aside, she was
who she was. And she needed time. Time for what? Time
for her to get her head on straight or time for her to make
his head spin to the point where he no longer knew which
way was up?

He stared at the phone a little longer, then searched for
and found his personal telephone directory, looking up an
old buddy from his school days, a friend who now owned
a rival stern-wheeler operation. He knew Tony Christinas
operated three boats and was constantly in need of help.
He also knew he needed to get back on the river—damn
the reasons—who cared on which boat? Having finally
made up his mind, he acted quickly.

For the first time since Megan had moved into the guest
house, John wasn't home when she got there. After the
disaster of the night before, she wasn't too surprised, but
she was terribly disappointed. She'd wanted to tell him that
she'd been wrong to run away, that whatever problems
they had should be faced. And she wanted to tell him that
she was not Betsy, that she wasn't even the same Megan,
that of course people can grow and change and maybe he
needed to start paying better attention.

Maybe that was why he was gone. Maybe the thought
of another scene with her was too much to handle.

She sighed heavily. All day she'd been silently rehearsing what words she could say or should say to make him understand. All day she'd been sick with the knowledge that there might not be any. He was deeply suspicious of her motives, that much was clear. He still thought she was looking to replace Robert!

Damn her subconscious—look at the nasty trick it had pulled the night before by pushing that loathsome man's image into her head, his name into her mouth, when all the time her heart was full of John Vermont.

Was he attracted to her because he saw her as a wounded bird that needed help and shelter? Isn't that how she had presented herself to him at first? Did he know it was no longer true? She had saved most of both paychecks; he had said he'd charge her rent eventually but never had. Should she move out now and prove to him that the least appealing thing about him was his money? He said a whole man wanted a whole woman, but she wasn't sure he was as healed as he claimed to be.

It didn't matter. She wasn't weak and needy and if he didn't like it, so be it. More than anything, she didn't want to lie to herself or to him. She had to somehow convince him that her feelings for him were real and that spats and setbacks were normal in the course of a relationship developing as quickly as theirs. They had to face them, not run away.

The memory of his kisses and his expert hands awakening her body came on suddenly and she plopped down onto the edge of the bed as she caught her breath. He was interested in making love to her, that much she was certain of. But was he willing to take the leap that would lead to this—the leap of faith in another human being? The leap of trust that she wasn't trying to trap him or use him? Without some leaping, loving was out of the question.

Bottom line—they needed to talk, openly and without equivocation. They needed to air their feelings. She got up from the bed and paced, anxious for him to come home.

But he didn't come. She waited until after dark and when he still wasn't back, she opened his front door with her key and switched on the light, worried that Lily might need to go outside. The dog was gone, too.

Without John, the empty house was like a cavern, never mind all the lights. The answering machine showed no blinking light that would indicate a message. It depressed her to be there, so she locked the door behind her and went to the guest house. She looked over the few grocery items she had on hand and decided to drive back to the River Rat and have dinner there.

The restaurant was an unequivocated dive that was a good thirty feet closer to the river than John's house. Inside, there was a bar along one wall and a dozen tables scattered across the rest of the building. A mirror behind the bar needed resilvering and was fronted by an uneven row of bottles. Four of the five stools were occupied by men who appeared to have been born right where they sat. The other one was empty.

Decorated in early riff-raff with a hazy layer of cigarette smoke and the smell of hot grease permeating everything, the joint was packed. Megan was approached by a middle-aged waitress wearing tight jeans and an apron printed with the picture of a beer-guzzling rat. Speculation weighed heavy in the woman's eyes as though she was used to knowing everyone who walked through the door and found it disconcerting when she couldn't place Megan.

"What can I do you for?" she asked.

"Dinner," Megan said, looking around the jammed restaurant.

The woman narrowed her eyes. "You've never been in here before, have you?"

"Nope. A…friend…recommended your place."

"No kidding. Well, we don't have a table empty right now. Who's your friend?"

"John Vermont," Megan said.

The woman's red lips spread into a wide smile. "Is that right? Hey, are you the girl he's got living with him?"

Megan said, "I'm his neighbor—more or less."

The woman winked. "My name is Shirl. Any friend of John's is a friend of mine."

"Well, thanks—"

"My, my. You're the first gal he's had since he threw Betsy out. Can you imagine a woman fooling around when she's got a stud like John Vermont at home in her bed?"

Well put, Megan thought. She said, with complete honesty, "No, I can't."

Shirl was clicking her tongue. "Me neither. He's enough to make a gal wish she wasn't already married. Anyway, we've all been curious about you."

Megan smiled faintly, suddenly wishing she'd stayed in the guest house and opened a can of chili.

Ushering her along to the empty stool, Shirl said, "Hey, you louts, sit up and look pretty. This girl is the reason we haven't been seeing as much of John Vermont as we used to."

One man looked at her with bleary eyes. "I heard you was a looker," he said with admiration.

"Uh, thanks," she said.

Another man added, "Boyd told us he'd seen you driving up and down the road. You'll find out, there ain't no secrets along the river."

"You make yourself comfortable, honey," Shirl said, almost pushing Megan up on the empty stool. "The boys here will take care of you till a table comes empty."

The man seated next to her shook his head. "John's been downright morose since Betsy hightailed it out of there. It's good to see him hooked up with a pretty girl like you."

"We're not really hooked up—"

"Don't mince words, sweetheart."

"Since you're a friend of John's, I'll buy you a beer," the third man said.

"Any friend of John's is a friend of ours," the bleary-eyed man added.

"What's your name?" the second man asked as a round of draft beer arrived with a basket of peanuts.

"Meg," she said without hesitation. For years the short-ening of her name had violated a childhood bond forged in grief, made between father and daughter. No wonder it had annoyed her when Robert used it to belittle her and empower himself. But last night John had used it with affection—for all the good it did them both—and in a way, he had given it back to her. "Meg," she repeated.

"Well, drink up, Meg, there's more where that came from! And take my advice, stay away from the fried shrimp. Old Billy ain't changed the grease for two months."

"I heard that!" a man in the restaurant behind her shouted.

The men laughed. Megan drank her beer.

She arrived back at John's house well before ten o'clock. His truck was still gone. It started raining again as she sat in her car and wondered if he'd run away from home. The other possibility—that he'd been in an accident or was hurt in some way—was too dreadful to contem-plate.

Again, she let herself into his house to check the an-swering machine. Nothing. Between the beer and the big bowl of clam chowder, her stomach was so full she ached. She collapsed on his sofa, just to sit for a second.

She awoke stiff and woozy. The house still felt empty. She got to her feet and once again checked his answering machine for a blinking light though she doubted she would have slept through a ringing phone.

Still nothing. That's when she finally noticed a folded

pair of sunglasses sitting on top of a pad of yellow paper. She was positive the glasses hadn't been there before she'd left for the River Rat, so John must have come home while she'd been away.

Well, apparently he wasn't worried about her, so why was she roaming around his empty house worrying about him? Locking the door behind her, she walked around to the guest house and found a piece of folded yellow paper inside a plastic sandwich bag tacked to her door.

She took it inside with her. "Megan," it said. "It's about eight-thirty and you aren't home. Don't worry when you find me gone. Lily is okay. See you sometime tomorrow. John."

So, he had been here while she was out yukking it up with his buddies. She undressed and put on the nightshirt he'd given her the first night she was here and which he'd refused to take back. She loved his nightshirt. It was huge, it was soft, and it was John's. She would have it forever and every time she wore it, she would think of him.

Well, their talk would have to take place tomorrow. She fell asleep as she practiced how to tell him she knew he was afraid of her and that sometimes she appeared to be fickle but really, truly, she knew exactly what she wanted and had for some time now. She wondered if, when hearing what she wanted was him, he'd run like a fox being pursued by a pack of dogs....

Megan arrived at the stern-wheeler to find Danny and a crew member stringing lights along the lower edge of the upper deck. Looking up at them from the dock, she called, "What are you guys doing?"

"Captain wants lights on each of the decks for the dinner cruise," Danny hollered.

She couldn't believe it. For some reason, she had a hard time picturing Norm Richardson caring about twinkling lights. She had to admit a grudging admiration for the idea; it certainly would look cheerful.

On the way to work, to keep herself from thinking too much about John, she'd reviewed the preparations for the party, which was less than two days away. After finding a warehouse manifest that included furniture, she'd talked to the foreman, making sure he understood they were to deliver two dozen circular tables for the dinner seating along with adequate linen and plush chairs for conversation areas. She had called the florist more times than she would ever admit to anyone, concerned that the table centerpieces and buffet table arrangements be flamboyant and original. Yes, yes, they assured her.

She'd ordered green plants from a nursery willing to rent them for a night and was mentally plotting where she would put them. The band that Agnes Colpepper had engaged was too pedantic for this crowd, so she'd paid out their option and arranged a replacement. All in all, the overall profit would be reduced, but if it went well, if these people were impressed, it could lead to more bookings and ultimately to more profit.

Besides, if she was going to be the unofficial hostess at this shindig, it was going to look sophisticated and come off as smooth as baby oil. Truth of the matter was, she'd been sidestepping Norm, hoping he didn't get whiff of all the extras—she dreaded trying to make him understand. And now, after all her careful steps to keep him uninvolved, he'd ordered little lights that would look enchanting once night fell. Who would have known?

She walked up the gangplank and lowered her umbrella. The weather was damp but warm and she found the rain more tolerable. Danny looked down at her from atop his ladder and said, "The captain wants to talk to you."

She inwardly groaned but said, "Okay."

"He said he'd wait for you in your cabin."

It took about five seconds for the implication to set in,

and Megan took off at a dead run across the deck and up the stairs. If Norm had found a way into her cabin, then he was in there with Foggy Dew and her kittens and all hell was about to break loose.

The door was unlocked and she tore it open. Sitting on the floor, Foggy Dew in his lap, the box of newborn kittens in front of him, was John Vermont.

Chapter Nine

It was like a tonic to her heart to see him sitting there cross-legged, grinning like a boy, holding his cat. She smiled at him warmly, but then she remembered why she'd come and her gaze searched the room for Norm.

John reached into the box and ran a fingertip down one tiny little gray nose. "Aren't they cute?"

She closed the door behind her. "They're absolutely precious," she said. "Where's Norm?"

John carefully put Foggy Dew back in the box with her family and rose to his feet in a fluid movement. "Gone," he said.

"But Danny told me the captain was in my office and wanted to see me—"

"I'm the captain," he said, looking down at her.

"You?"

"Well, it's my boat, isn't it?"

"Yes—"

"And when someone quits, I'm stuck filling in," he said, his eyes dancing.

"Are you saying Norm quit?"

"Are you disappointed?"

"No," she said immediately. "Heavens no."

"Good."

They were standing very close to each other, and Megan found talking to him a bit more daunting than she had anticipated. There was something kind of reckless and brisk about him today, something that kept her from launching into an emotional dialogue about trust and feelings. Instead, she wanted to kiss him, wanted *him* to kiss *her*, just so their lips would be pressed together.

"Where were you last night?" he asked.

"At the River Rat with your cronies, drinking beer and eating peanuts till the wee hours," she said.

His eyes grew wide. "You met Les and Boyd?"

She reveled in making him look so shocked. "And Kit and Shirl and some guy with bleary eyes."

"O'Donnell. My, my. They must have loved meeting you."

"They all obviously care a lot about you."

"They're great people, but you can't believe everything they tell you."

She thought of the way they'd all mentioned Betsy, and how her leaving had thrown John. She wouldn't tell him this. She said, "They were all very nice."

"I bet they were."

"Where were you?"

"I spent the night here," he said.

"And where is Lily?"

"She's in my cabin. I decided if I was going to be here every day, she could be here, too."

"What about her predilection for chasing cats?"

"We'll work it out," he said.

She narrowed her eyes. "Are you moving aboard the boat?"

"Heavens no," he said, echoing her earlier response.

"Then why did you stay here?"

He stared at her long enough to make her nervous about what he might say. "You want the truth?" he finally asked.

What she wanted was a good lungful of air; it was hard to get enough with his eyes piercing hers like that. Was he completely ignorant of the way he made her feel? Couldn't he sense her desire for him? She said, "I guess so…"

"I thought we could use a night apart," he said, averting his gaze.

Inwardly she laughed, but it was hollow. So he *had* run away from home! She said, "If one of us is going to leave your house, don't you think it makes more sense for it to be me?"

This brought his eyes back to her face. "Who said anything about one of us leaving the house? I just thought that after the other night, it might be a good idea to spend a little time apart. So I came here and you went to the River Rat."

To wait for you, she thought. *To tell you so many things….*

"Anyway," he continued. "We have two weddings today but nothing tomorrow."

"Tomorrow we get ready for the media dinner-dance."

"I thought we had an excursion in the morning."

"We did," she admitted. "I rescheduled it. I just couldn't see how we could get everything ready for this blasted party if we were out on the river."

He rubbed the back of his neck. "So we lost a paying account?"

"No, we delayed one account to make sure we did a proper job on coming through for another paying account, one that might mean the beginning of a new market for this ship."

"We don't need new markets," he mumbled.

His attitude made her want to scream at him. He hated

anyone telling him anything about anything, she knew that. He hated change. He didn't trust her, not with his heart and not with his precious boat. Keeping all this tension out of her voice, she said, "Of course we do. It's important to the future of the stern-wheeler."

"And why do you suddenly care about the future of the stern-wheeler?" he asked, his expression making it very clear that he doubted her motives were anything but self-serving.

The annoyance turned to hurt. "My concern is not sudden—I've been thinking about things like this since you first gave me this job. I like the old barge."

"Your fiancé's term."

"My *ex*-fiancé." She softened a little as she added, "*I* use the term with affection. Kind of the way you used my nickname the other night."

His stare was now laserlike. He finally said, "What happened the other night was...ill-advised, Megan. You must have noticed by now that I have a hard time when it comes to controlling myself around you. I promise you, it won't happen again. You were right to walk away."

"I didn't walk away because you kissed me," she informed him.

He looked extremely uncomfortable. "I know," he said.

Again they stared. Finally he shook his head. "Back to important things. You are planning on being here for the dinner-dance, right? I can depend on you?"

Despite the fact that she felt like smacking him upside the head, she wished he would take her in his arms and do some ill-advised kissing. "If you can face Robert, so can I," she said. *This* was more important than talking about what was happening between them?

"I half hope he starts something."

"You talk tough," she said.

"Yeah. Well, truth of the matter is, I'll be my usual good-humored self. I think we should bring a change of clothes tomorrow and dress for the party here on the boat. What do you think?''

I think I'm going to go nuts if we don't stop acting like a couple of robots! ''That sounds good,'' she said. The room was growing so stuffy she was having trouble thinking. She kept hearing him say they needed distance. It sounded as if he was going to tell her to get lost. Should she quit before he humiliated her by firing her? She was racked with misery and indecision…this just wasn't going the way she had planned. She had to get out of here. Grasping at the first thought that came to mind, she added, ''I'm going to go downstairs to wash the windows on the observation deck. I noticed they're smudged.''

''I'll get one of the deckhands to help you,'' he said as they moved toward the door. Their hands touched as they both reached for the knob, and in unison, they jerked back and waited for the other to go ahead and open the door.

Hitching his hands on his waist and staring down at her, he said, ''We need to talk, don't we?''

At last. ''Yes.''

''I keep thinking about what you said, how you needed time. I think you're right, I think that's exactly what you need.''

She stared at him. She wasn't sure what to say or what to think.

''Listen,'' he continued, ''let's just get through this damn dinner thing and then we'll talk about what comes next.''

''And what happened two nights ago,'' she insisted. ''You need to understand…I need to explain—''

''That's history,'' he said.

''And you don't like to address history, do you?'' she snapped.

''Not particularly.''

Maybe this whole thing is hopeless… She actually found herself wishing Norm Richardson was here! She opened the door and preceded John into the walkway. "Did Norm say why he quit?"

"He got a better job offer."

"I'm sorry."

"You are?"

"I know how much you hate being here."

"I'll live," he said.

"You're the one who ordered the little lights to be strung, aren't you?" she added.

"Yes. Do you approve?"

"Very much so."

"I saw a brown sack in the closet by the box with the kittens in it and I thought it might contain cat food, so I looked," he said.

Megan bit her bottom lip. "The cat food is in the bottom drawer of the file cabinet."

"I found your disposable cameras in the bag. Why aren't they down below on sale?"

She tilted her chin defiantly. "Because Norm thought it was a stupid idea, just like you did."

"I didn't think it was a stupid idea," he protested.

"You sure acted as though you did. When I mentioned it, your face got all sour."

"No—"

"Yes, it did. Every time I tried to do something different, from bringing the children to your wheelhouse to instigating weekend brunch cruises, you let me know how awful you thought it was. And after all, it's your boat, right?"

"It didn't stop you from rescheduling tomorrow's excursion, did it?"

"It just made me sneaky," she said.

The last wedding of the day took place under an awning as warm rain came down in torrents. The bride was young, no more than twenty, and the groom was twice her age.

Both their families looked resigned to the union but not particularly pleased. The man next to Megan was videotaping the event.

She didn't think she'd be present for many more weddings, so she paid attention to the words this time. This took a lot of concentration, as always before, she'd gotten so wrapped up in John's delivery that she'd ignored the message. And with Norm, she'd donned figurative earplugs so as not to nod off while he droned on and on.

Love. Honor. Respect. Fidelity. Eternity. Huge words with huge meanings. How lightly she'd agreed to these very concepts with Robert at her side. How blithely she'd stood here and taken these tremendous commitments without actually giving them a second thought. In retrospect, it was almost as if the hand of God had reached down and made Robert kick the cat overboard as a wake-up call. How thankful she was that she'd listened.

She studied John's face as he looked from the woman to the man. She watched his lips move, saw him mentally measure the two, and knew what he was thinking. A man who has worked his way to where he is, who has reached forty years and a decent bank balance, who has experienced some of the joys and the miseries of life—marrying a woman who was a teenager only yesterday, a child, untested, fresh, lovely to behold…a danger and a heartache wearing a white gown.

I love you… The thought came suddenly, like a jolt from heaven above, but it settled almost instantly in her heart as though it had sprung from the deepest recesses of her being. *I love you. I love your eyes. I love your nose. I love the way you speak and the way you listen. I love your stubborn streak and your self-delusions and your wit. I even love and accept your weaknesses.*

As his straight dark hair ruffled in the slight breeze moving through the awning, his tall figure so resolute and unflappable, John raised his eyes. For an instant she was sure her feelings were written on her face, for a flicker of concern settled on his brow.

And suddenly she knew that to him she was an attractive nuisance, the kind of thing insurance companies write policies for. She was a Betsy or even this young bride…an ill-advised distraction who didn't even know her own mind.

She felt warm tears roll down her cheeks and she dropped her gaze. Beside her, the video camera rolled along, recording the ceremony, catching John's image. She wondered if she could get a copy of it so she would have him forever, at least on tape. She wanted only the best for him; she needn't be part of his life as long as he was happy.

Lies. What she wanted was for him to be struck by the same jolt that had singed her heart. She wanted him to love her. She wanted the impossible.

It was time to leave. Time to find a new job with new possibilities. Time to find a new place to live. Time to find a man who could admit he liked children and wasn't so bitter about women, who could see her for who she was at that moment, not hold her past against her. She would do everything in her power to make sure John wasn't left worse off because he'd known her. She would help him control their mutual attraction so that his heart wouldn't have to mend again. She would leave him with bookings for his boat so he'd be busy. And somehow, she would take care of Robert's threats of a lawsuit.

The man next to her tapped her arm. "Excuse me, miss. Would you hold this camera while I find another battery in my case? This one is fading fast. Just keep pointing it over there."

"Sure," she said, taking the video camera. As soon as she looked through the viewfinder, she recalled another video camera, another day, and a smile spread across her lips.

The man nudged her again. "Found it," he said, and she handed him back his camera. "Thanks," he added.

"My pleasure," she said, still smiling. She was the one who should be thanking him!

The stern-wheeler had never looked better. The three rows of tiny white lights shone bravely through the rain. Groupings of chairs made discreet by the green plants gave the boat the look of a good hotel. The round tables, covered with white damask cloths, boasted a truly original floral centerpiece fashioned around an oil lamp. The lamps were now lit and their soft glow made the main salon look wonderful.

John had informed her right as she got back from a quick trip downtown, that he wasn't going to move the boat tonight. The coast guard had closed the river due to floating debris and the dumping of melted snow—a result of warm winds earlier in the day—into the already-swollen river. Night navigation of the Willamette would be too dangerous.

She didn't care and she doubted whether any of the party-goers would care, either.

She ducked into her cabin, dumped her new purchase on the sofa, said a soft hello to Foggy Dew and the kittens, and stripped off her jeans and sweatshirt. She took a quick shower, brushed her unruly hair and applied her makeup.

The dress she'd chosen was another from her unused trousseau, a long black chemise with a daring neckline and spaghetti straps. She fastened on silver earrings and a chunky silver bracelet, then tried to catch enough of her reflection in the tiny mirror to see if she looked pulled together. At the last second she slipped into black heels, knowing her feet would be sending her hate mail before an hour had passed.

John's cabin door was open, Lily sitting sentinel in the middle of the doorway. She woofed and wagged when she saw Megan, who sidestepped the shedding yellow mutt. She placed the VCR tape she'd bought in town out of the way on top of the television just as John stepped out of the head, running a hand through his hair, glancing at her as he came into view. He looked incredible in his formal black uniform that boasted no fancy buttons or decals or insignias, just yards of black wool encasing a very tall, very strong, very sexy man.

"Wow," he said, staring at her.

"Ditto," she said. He was looking at her the way he had twice before when they'd ended up in each other's arms. She had never been looked at this way, as though she was nourishment, as though she was more precious than water to a man dying of thirst, as though every detail of her face was being committed to memory to be savored in the future. It was disconcerting, to say the least.

"You're doing it again," she managed to say.

"What?" he asked, moving closer.

"Looking at me."

She had to lean her head back to peer into his eyes. He was near enough he could easily embrace her and she throbbed with the desire for him to do so. Instead, hands at his side, he said, "I promised you, remember? I won't touch you. But I can still look. Or would you rather I didn't?"

"No," she mumbled, just about at the point where she couldn't form a word to save her life.

He broke the spell with a smile. "Don't worry, Megan, you're safe with me. If I touch you at all, it will be on the dance floor. Deal?"

"Deal," she said, her insides suddenly on fire at the thought of dancing with John beneath the stars—well, beneath the rain clouds—of being held tightly in his arms. With a surge of hope, she wondered if they could find a way to get past the other night.

* * *

Along with the committee that had arranged the party, Megan greeted the two hundred and twenty-one guests with a practiced smile that she prayed hid her acute embarrassment over knowing that at least twenty percent of them had actually been at her almost wedding and the rest had heard all the gory details.

As John stood across from her, shaking hands and making small talk with an adeptness that surprised—and fascinated—her, she worked at handling the curious stares, the hushed remarks, the overt questions that a few brave souls dared to ask.

"Have you seen Robert since…well, you know…"

"Hey, is Winslow still all wet?"

"Oh, honey, you must be mortified to be here…"

"Megan, I want you to know I think you're so brave to face everyone after…well, you know…"

"Yes," she wanted to scream, "I know, I know!"

But she didn't. Between waves of party-goers, she found her eyes straying to John. She was cognizant of the fact that not only was almost every female in the room aware of him as a man, but that there was also heavy speculation concerning Megan's and John's relationship. She couldn't blame that on him, however, as he hadn't looked her way since coming down to the main salon. It was her gaze that wandered.

The bright note was that as the first thirty minutes passed and Robert didn't arrive, she began to hope she at least wouldn't have to face him. Maybe he would use his considerable common sense to know that he should avoid this boat and the eager eyes that anticipated a confrontation.

Danny, who had collected and counted the tickets, announced that there were fewer than a dozen no-shows. Megan smiled to herself as she noticed a pretty intern from one of the television stations waiting in the wings for Danny to finish his report to John.

The party organizers had dispersed and cocktails had begun when she began to realize she could relax, she was home-free. Within seconds of her first sigh of relief, Robert arrived, forty minutes later, a striking redhead on his arm. Megan kicked herself for forgetting how he liked to arrive after everyone else so that he would be the focus. As usual, he managed to draw attention to himself like a magnet at a heavy metal concert as he strode into the salon like some kind of conquering hero.

Megan was aware of a few gasps around her as Robert came to a stop right in front of her. She planted a huge smile on her face and, taking a deep breath, stretched out a hand. "Hello, Robert, welcome to the *Ruby Rose*."

He threw back his head and laughed, ignoring her hand, his arm now draped across the redhead's bare shoulders. He said, "You work here, bring us a drink. What'll it be, Fontaine, champagne?"

Fontaine had a throaty voice and brown eyes that were as flat as the river on a still day. She said, "I adore champagne."

Robert fixed Megan with an icy stare. "You heard the lady, get her some champagne. Oh, and you know what I like, only make it a double."

Suddenly, Megan, who was about to swallow her pride and get these two jerks a drink—anything just to escape this public forum—was aware of a growing heat behind her and she knew without turning that John had approached.

Looking over her shoulder, she met his gaze and a million nebulous impressions passed between them in an instant.

Nodding at Robert and his guest, John said, "Nice to have you both aboard." She knew him well enough to tell from his voice that he was anything but pleased to be welcoming Robert.

"I want you to meet my attorney," Robert said, "Fontaine Montague of Montague and Hindle. You've heard of her, I assume."

John shook her hand. "Of course," he said. "Well, folks, there's an open bar right over there in the corner and two trays of champagne floating about somewhere."

"Fontaine specializes in personal-injury cases," Winslow said, ignoring John's gesture to move to the bar.

The lady lawyer licked her upper lip as she stared at John. It appeared to Megan, who was amazed to find she was jealous, that it looked as though the attorney was plotting a way to settle the dispute out of court...as long as it was done in private with John!

"I see," John said.

Fontaine cracked a little smile, the first Megan had seen. "Robert has been telling me what a fiasco you had on board a few weeks ago. We'll have to talk next week and see what we can do about it."

A knot showed up in John's jaw, but he kept his civility as he said, "It sounds as though I need to contact my lawyer."

Fontaine tilted her head and regarded John. "That might not be necessary," she said slowly. "Why don't we just have a friendly...chat...first."

This elicited a short bark of laughter. "Sorry, Miss Montague, but it's been my experience that friendly chats with lawyers can be quite costly, so you just call ahead and I'll get Walter Green here, as well."

"If that's the way you want it," she said, the sex kitten gone, the barracuda back.

John turned his attention to Megan. "Tyler mentioned he'd like your help down in the galley."

Megan had no idea why the cook would want to speak with her. She took a small step away, lingering.

John turned his attention back to Robert and said, "Allow me to show you folks where the bar is."

Robert elbowed John away. "We can find the bar, sailor

boy. You'd better just go call your lawyer friend—you're going to need all the representation you can get."

"I'm shaking in my boots," John said with a grin.

Fontaine nodded politely as she led Robert, who was nearly apoplectic, away.

John looked down at Megan. "Suppose anyone would really miss that man if he just turned up missing one day?"

"I seriously doubt it. Why, do you have plans?"

"Just dreams," he said with a wicked smile.

She touched his sleeve. "All joking aside, Robert could make big trouble for you."

"We'll see." He stared down into her eyes and added, "You are saving a dance for me?"

She smiled. She'd been saving a dance for him since the first day she was aboard this boat.

Danny showed up at John's elbow. "There's a group of radio people who want a tour of the wheelhouse," he said.

John nodded, then looked back at Megan. "Duty calls."

She watched him walk away, a head taller than most everyone else, his shoulders broad, his back straight, and felt almost faint with desire. Maybe she was safe with him, but she couldn't guarantee he was safe with her.

She sat on the small chair in the stainless-steel galley, nibbling on vegetable sticks she'd swiped from a passing tray, while Tyler directed his help in a ballet of movements designed to get the hot foods onto the buffet table while they were still hot. He looked at her at last and said, "But I never asked to see you."

"The captain said…"

"I haven't even seen Captain Vermont since this afternoon when he was down here making himself a sandwich. I don't know what you're talking about. You must be mistaken."

But she wasn't mistaken and she knew it. She also knew what John had done and that was to attempt to rescue her from Robert and Fontaine Montague. She supposed she should be grateful, but what she was, was angry.

This was just another example of how he felt about her—that he was supposed to find some way to make her life easier by shouldering the responsibility himself. Well, she didn't need his help. She got up from the chair and left the galley, ducking between the platters and tureens, determined to find John and tell him what she thought.

When she finally found him, however, he was on the stern in the midst of giving what had to be his second tour. He caught Megan's eye and winked as he told the gathered throng that the boat had two rudders for maneuvering, that the paddle weighed eighteen tons and drew a foot of water while the boat itself drew four feet. "Some of the old paddle wheelers had a draft of only six inches," he told them. "People said that on a good dew, you could take the boat right through the front yard."

Now was not the time to throw a tantrum, it was time to work. She went back inside the salon. Danny met her at the door and took her elbow. "The old boat has never looked better, Megan, you're a real magician. And I've had four separate parties ask about renting it for similar occasions. I told them to call you first thing in the morning."

Megan smiled. She felt proud her work had apparently paid off—and disappointed John hadn't seen fit to pass along the same kind of compliments.

Robert was holding court with a few of his buddies, entertaining them with his plans to sue John and own "this leaky barge" within a year once his lawyer got through with him. Megan watched as the lady lawyer apparently grew weary of trying to tone down her client's monologue and left the ship.

As Megan and Danny helped people through the buffet line, Robert's threats and boasts droned on in the background. She knew most of what he said was fueled by multiple gin and cranberries. She also knew that even if only half of what he threatened came true, he would ruin this boat for John.

A vision assaulted her. Tugboats residing on the river, once John's, sold to pay off Betsy. And this stern-wheeler, rotting at her pilings, once John's, taken by Megan's jilted fiancé for no better reason than wounded pride.

No. She simply couldn't allow it to happen. It was time to implement the plan she'd first thought of two days before when the man next to her had asked her to hold his camcorder. She waited until Robert's audience was down to three or four listeners, and approached him.

"I need to speak with you," she said.

He winked at her. "I told you it was too late," he said, his voice even. Robert didn't get sloppy drunk, he just got mean.

"I have something I want to show you," she told him.

He looked intrigued. He put a hand on her arm and said, "Maybe I can make an exception, Meg."

"Good," she said, smiling, ignoring the way the feel of his hand made her skin crawl. "You'll have to come with me," she added.

This elicited a broad wink and an answering bevy of snorts and titters from his buddies, but he followed her out onto the deck.

What weathermen were calling a pineapple express had been blowing since noon, and Megan welcomed the moist but warm air that lifted her hair and freshened her skin. Robert grabbed her as soon as they were away from the portholes and, hovering over her, breathed gin-tainted breath on her face. "Is this what you had in mind?" he asked, his lips against her cheek.

She pushed him away, half hoping he'd stumble and fall off the boat again. He didn't. "Don't touch me," she said. "Just follow."

"You've never looked sexier," he said, lunging toward her again.

She sidestepped him and darted up the stairs. She could hear his footsteps behind her and suddenly doubted the wisdom of this plan. As obnoxious as Robert had been in the past, she'd never felt threatened by him. Of course, before she'd crossed him, he'd never presented this side of himself.

By the time Robert caught up with her, she was opening the door to John's cabin. Lily wagged her tail happily at the unexpected company until she caught sight of Robert, whom she greeted with a deep growl.

Only went to show the dog had good taste when it came to sizing up a man. On the other hand, she didn't need Lily actually tasting Robert's ankle and risking another messy lawsuit, so she coaxed the animal into the head and closed the door.

Robert made a new pass at her, but she slipped away. She pulled out one of the chairs from around John's table and said, "Please, Robert, just sit there. I want to show you something."

He tugged on his vest and slicked back his hair as though it had suddenly occurred to him he'd been acting like a junior high school kid. Megan was very relieved when he sat down as she directed.

She inserted the tape of their ill-fated wedding day into the VCR and turned on the television. Then, taking the remote, sat in a chair, as well.

There had been no time to review the tape and see what the cameraman had actually recorded so she was forced to sit there and hope for the best.

"What in the hell kind of trick is this?" Robert bellowed.

"Remember how we hired a man to tape our wedding? Just watch," she said, startled with the first images of herself that flicked across the screen. What she saw was a scared-looking waif wearing an elaborate gown and a nervous smile. And look at the way she stared at John, as though using him to find the internal courage it took to stand next to Robert and complete her vows. She felt as though she'd moved a million years and a million miles away from the woman on the tape.

"Meg, you've had your fun and games. I don't think this is amusing."

"Neither do I," she said, pointing at the monitor. "Watch, right here is where you kick Foggy Dew. See!" She rewound the last few seconds of the tape and played it over again.

"What the hell—"

"Just watch," she said again. The tape caught everything from Robert kicking the little cat to John and Megan rushing to the side and then down the stairs to the lower deck. It caught John casting the life ring and then straddling the deck as he pulled on the safety line, and Robert snarling, and Megan pushing Robert into the river. And then there was the rescue of the cat first and Robert second, more insults and threats, right up to the point where Robert called the video man an imbecile and ordered him to quit taping.

It ended abruptly. Robert stared at the blank screen, silent. As Megan rewound the tape, she said, "There are several copies of this. I'm prepared to make it available to all those television people down there right after I show them the kittens that the cat you kicked into the river managed to deliver safely. I should warn you, they are exceptionally cute kittens and will photograph well. Imagine yourself on the local news. 'Prominent businessman lashes out at kitty mom-to-be! Tape at eleven.' Maybe the national news will pick it up as a human interest story. And the tabloids—"

"That's enough," he said, standing. Reaching for his checkbook, he added, "What do you want?"

Megan stood, too. It was important to her to face him eye-to-eye. She said, "I want you to drop any and all legal action against this boat and John Vermont for now and into the future. I won't hesitate to use this tape if I have to, and that's a promise."

"Is that all?" he asked.

"That's all."

Megan could tell he thought she was a fool for asking for so little. She had no intention of letting him know that she'd actually asked for everything she wanted—John's peace of mind and no embarrassing scenes in a courtroom.

He put a hand on her shoulder and stared at her. "You've changed," he said at last.

"I sincerely hope so."

He nodded. Before she knew what he was doing, he had leaned down and kissed her mouth. For just an instant she wondered if his kiss would mean anything to her. It meant less than nothing, she was relieved to discover. Much less than nothing.

She pulled away, smiling, kind of anxious to inform Robert that he could go on his merry way now and forget she ever existed. A movement off to the left caught her eye and she turned, startled to find John standing in the doorway.

The look in his eyes was enough to know that he'd witnessed, and misinterpreted, Robert's kissing her. She took a step toward him but Robert caught her arm and pulled her back. Waving the checkbook in the air, he said, "How much do you want this time, Meg, the same as before?"

She tore herself away from Robert's grasp and turned to find that John was gone.

"Why, Robert?" she asked, turning back. "Why did you do that to me?"

Robert smiled smugly. "Payback time, baby." As he put his checkbook away, he chuckled. "Did you see the look on your brave old captain's face? It looks as though you've lost another sugar daddy.''

Before Megan left the cabin, she threw all her weight behind her right arm and punched Robert Winslow in the mouth.

Chapter Ten

John found himself at the bow, hands grasping the line, head bent, eyes focused on the wet deck, warm rain pounding the back of his neck. The sound of music wafted up from the dance floor below, mingling with the sound of raindrops hitting the deck.

He felt molten lava flowing through his veins—it hurt in a way he'd almost forgotten, with a searing, biting pain that made his breath short.

Well, of course it hurt! She'd made a fool of him. How long had she been stringing both of them along? The nerve of that woman, the unmitigated nerve! *He should have known....*

And she'd smiled. It was a different smile than he'd ever seen on her face, a knowing smile, the smile a woman makes when she realizes what it is she wants, who it is she wants. She'd kissed Winslow and then she'd smiled and in some ways, the smile was worse than the kiss...

And for this he'd connived and manipulated Norm off the boat and into another position aboard another stern-wheeler? For this he'd come back?

"There you are," she said. He heard the click of her heels as she crossed the deck. She stopped right next to him. All he could see were her black shoes and the turn of her pretty ankles. He closed his eyes.

"John..." she began, but he cut her off.

"Don't try to justify what you've been doing," he said.

"What *I've* been doing?" she asked, and damned if her voice didn't sound incredulous.

"Money aside, you kissed him, Megan," he said, looking at her through the corners of his eyes. The rain had flattened her hair against her skull and her wet skin glistened in the deck lights. He steeled himself against her appeal, which was just as strong—and misplaced—as ever.

"Correction," she said. "*He* kissed me."

"What's the difference?"

She pulled on his arm. "At least face me," she demanded.

"Why?"

"You're accusing me of taking money from Robert and then kissing him. The least you can do is look me in the eye."

"I don't have the stomach to look you in the eye," he said.

"You think I liked him kissing me," she said, the incredulous tone back.

He strained and did what she asked. He faced her. "I saw you smile, Megan. I *know* you liked it."

She nodded, her mouth a tight line, ashamed, he guessed, at having been caught. He added, "All along you've known I was reluctant to get involved with you, so you've been making sure Winslow wasn't out of the picture."

She seemed to be trembling despite the fact that it was almost seventy degrees. "Is that what you think?"

"*That's* what I know."

She looked positively grim. His guess was that she had

wanted to keep him dangling just in case Winslow bolted. As angry as he was with her, he was also hurt and betrayed and he yearned for her to somehow convince him he was wrong, that despite what he'd seen with his own eyes, it hadn't gone down the way he thought.

Instead she said, "You make me sad, John Vermont, but mostly what you make me is mad."

"*I* make *you* mad!" Now he was incredulous.

"You know what? You want to believe I was kissing Robert to try to get him back because then I'd live up to the image you have of me, the image, thanks to that rotten old Betsy, that you have of all women."

"Don't try to turn this around," he warned her.

"And you positively adore thinking I was taking money from him because that also fits your image of a woman!" She hit him on the chest with both fists. "I am not Betsy," she said vehemently. She pounded on him again, tears mixing with raindrops on her face. "There are dozens of ways we're not alike, haven't you noticed? Or are you so blinded by your past that you can't see?"

He held her fists in his hands. "I can see, all right," he said. "I can see that you've got Winslow back where you want him—"

She shoved him against the railing, but he pulled her along with him. "I do not have Robert back, nor do I want him back. What you saw was Robert kissing me for some perverted reason I don't even want to think about—"

"But you smiled, I saw it—"

"I smiled because his kiss was pointless, meaningless, less than nothing. I was glad I'd grown past him."

"You were in my cabin—"

"Because I showed him a videotape of our wedding that clearly shows him making a fool out of himself by kicking Foggy Dew over the side of the boat. I threatened to show it to all the media people aboard if he didn't leave you alone!"

Her words took a second to sink in. As they did, it was like a cool rain dousing a brushfire. He wanted to hear this. He wanted to believe it. As the seconds passed, it all began to make sense, it all fit with the woman he'd come to know. It was as though he'd been partially insane for a while, acting on instinct, hotheaded, heartsick...

Her wet body was pressed against him, and suddenly he found himself lifting her off her feet and kissing her mouth with a wild abandon that shot arrows of desire to all parts of his body and heart. He held on to her so tightly his arms ached as the fire so recently extinguished came back in a flash and he felt consumed by it, deliriously consumed. And for an instant, she was his, he could tell.

But she pushed herself away with a force that startled him, skidding back, almost falling in her rush to get away from him. He reached out to steady her and she pushed him away again. One high heel broke and she stood in the rain, a little lopsided. "I have half a mind to shove *you* overboard," she said through chattering teeth as she held on to the rail.

"It wouldn't be the first time you shoved a man into the river."

She tore off her broken shoe and threw it over the side. "Don't you joke with me! Do you think your kisses are so wonderful that you can accuse me of lying to you and betraying whatever the hell it is we have between us and then change your mind and take it all back just like that?"

"No, but—"

"Robert thought I could be bought," she said, ditching the other shoe. "When that didn't work, he decided to humiliate me and hurt me, but that wouldn't have worked, either, if you hadn't so willingly taken his bait. *You* still think I can be bought. You're no better than Robert Winslow!"

"Now, that's just plain nasty!"

"You just keep your hands to yourself."

He grabbed her shoulders. "Megan—"

"I have had it with men!" she said, twisting away from his grip.

"You don't mean that!"

"Don't I?"

He held out a hand of entreaty, but she'd disappeared behind the wheelhouse and was gone. He felt like one of those houses that gets caught in a hurricane, torn from its foundation and deposited ten miles away.

The music taunted him. He was supposed to be dancing with her, holding her, telling her that after a little time, well, who knew....

Swearing, he shook himself off like Lily would and, shoes squashing, went to get everyone the hell off his boat.

Megan took off her ruined dress. It wasn't the first water-soaked gown she'd had to deep-six on this blasted boat and the irony of it only fueled the anger and the ultimate emptiness in her heart. Wiping hot tears from her face, she looked through the few clothes she had aboard, anxious to find something warm to chase away the bone-numbing chill she couldn't shake.

She pulled on jeans and a bulky sweater. She'd just towel-dried her hair and combed it back from her forehead when she heard a soft knock and knew it was John. She wanted to tell him to go away, but this time she wasn't going to avoid him or run. She said, "Come in."

The door swung open but he stayed in the open frame. "Everyone is gone but the staff who are cleaning up."

She didn't say a word.

"People were very excited about the boat," he continued. "I think your idea worked, that lots of bookings will come from this." A lengthy pause was followed by the words, "Thanks Megan."

"You're welcome," she said stiffly as she bunched her belongings together and tossed them in a box. "I'll be out of here in a minute or two. I'll move out of your house tomorrow. I've been thinking. There's this girl where I use to work named Melanie Smith. I happen to know she hates her job. I think she'd be just right.''

He wrinkled his forehead. ''For what?''

''To take over my job. I'm leaving.''

''Oh,'' he said. He was still wearing his dark uniform, which was wet and clung to his shoulders like a second skin. His hair glistened in the overhead light, so black it had blue streaks. He was big and strong and Megan had no idea how she could love someone and hate him all at the same time, all in the same breath.

No, what she felt wasn't hate, she realized as she pulled on socks. It was disappointment. She didn't measure up in his eyes, and he didn't measure up in hers, not in the ways it counted, not in the ways that went with the huge words he pontificated every day. Love, honor, fidelity, trust, eternity. Saying them wasn't enough—you had to feel them, too.

''I'll drive you home,'' he said, turning to open his cabin door. Lily shuffled across the walkway and licked Megan's hand.

That's when it struck her that they had driven in together, that she'd borrowed his truck to run into town, that she was stuck on this boat once again with no transportation other than a ride from John.

''It'll give us a chance to talk,'' he added.

Lily had immediately found the box of kittens and was sniffing them gently, tail wagging, as Foggy Dew rubbed herself around the dog's legs. Well, at least *they* could be friendly. The life she was about to lose—work on this boat, her plans and dreams here, these animals she'd come to treasure, this man she couldn't help loving—suddenly seemed so precious that she found a new wave of bitter tears flooding her eyes, spilling down her cheeks.

"I can't go with you," she said softly, dropping her deck shoes.

He shook his head. "Megan—"

"No, John, I mean it." She couldn't face talking with him. She had an idea what talking would lead to... concessions, his arms. His complete lack of faith in her still stung.

He just stared at her.

"I guess I should ask your permission, after all, it's your boat."

"Yes, it is," he said, irritation darkening his eyes. "But no, you go ahead and hide out here if you want."

"I'm not hiding," she snapped.

"Aren't you?"

"No. I'm avoiding being alone with you."

"I told you you'd be safe. I also told you I was sorry I misjudged you."

"You never said that," Megan said.

He paused, appearing to think back. Finally he said, "I kissed you. It's the same thing, isn't it?"

"It most assuredly is not," she said firmly.

"You know the trouble with you, Megan Morison? You don't know what you want."

He was wrong; she knew exactly what she wanted. That was the trouble. Touching his hand, she said, "You know the trouble with you, John Vermont? You can't imagine why any woman would love you if not for your money, and that's really stupid." With that, she shooed Lily out and closed the door. Leaning back against it, she let the tears roll down her cheeks.

John awoke with a start. Lily was camped out on the foot of his bed, half her considerable weight on top of his legs. He gruffly told her to move over. But it wasn't the dog that had awakened him.

It was that woman! As the rain pounded on his roof, he

thought about everything that had happened last night, reconstructing all the events in sequence. He could see now where he'd acted like a jerk. He couldn't understand why he'd so quickly believed the insinuations of a man he loathed unless Megan was right, unless deep in the dark corners of his black heart, he wanted to believe those bad things about her so he could wash his hands of her before she washed her hands of him.

Now, he thought, how sick is this?

About as sick as using Betsy to judge Megan. It was like taking a cracked plate into a store and rejecting a perfect one because it wasn't right. It was like taking a hammer and pounding on the new plate until it finally cracked and then sitting back and saying, "Aha, I knew all plates were flawed!"

He got to his feet and paced the room. Oh, the scenarios he had fantasized about over the weeks, with Megan only a stone's throw away. A thousand times he'd imagined the look of her face on his pillow, the smell of her hair when he folded her into his arms, the soft laughter, the deep sighs...

All this stuff took trust and he'd blown it big time. Over and over again, he'd refused to believe she could care about him for any other reason than his bank account. Had Betsy left him so insecure?

Good heavens, *he* was the cracked plate!

He stood with his head against the wall, his arms hanging loosely by his sides, trying to think. She'd said the trouble with him was that he couldn't imagine a woman loving him for more than his money. Where had the word *love* come from? They'd never talked about love before. Why did he always feel as though he was three steps behind her?

The rain pounded so hard it became part of his brain waves. And then, with another start, he realized it was noise that had awakened him.

A premonition so real it had shape instantly filled his mind. Throwing on his jeans and shoes, he ran bare chested out into the night, Lily on his heels, a powerful flashlight in his hands. It was still warm with a faint breeze blowing, and the premonition now spilled over into his body, hastening his movements. He ran to the edge of the patio, shone his light down the slope and saw the answering twinkle of water many feet higher than it was supposed to be—all the way up to the landing where he'd last held Megan in his arms.

The dock was gone. His skiff was gone. The river was flooding and Megan was alone on the stern-wheeler.

Heart racing, he ran back inside and tried to use the phone, but the line was dead. Grabbing his jacket and the keys by the door, he ran outside. A tree had fallen, partially blocking the driveway, taking down his telephone pole. Its roots unable to cling to the sodden earth, the budding branches had missed his truck by less than a foot. Maybe the tree crashing to the ground was the noise that had awakened him.

Lily jumped into the passenger seat, excited and nervous. Hell, so was he. The windshield wipers slammed back and forth in time with his heartbeat. When he passed the River Rat, his headlights revealed that half the restaurant and several power poles were gone—washed away. Thank God it was the middle of the night and the joint was empty. He gunned the engine and headed to Portland.

He passed people frantically sandbagging their homes and emergency vehicles and television news vans. The wharf area was partially flooded so he flung the truck into four-wheel drive and, heedless of signs warning of high water, raced through puddles wider than swimming holes and almost as deep.

At last he was at the pier. Leaving the truck lights on so he could see, taking the flashlight again, he and Lily ran out as far as they could, then stopped, shining the light back and forth in ever-increasing arcs.

The pier was gone...and so was the stern-wheeler. And so, his heart cried, was Megan....

Megan partially awoke when Foggy Dew jumped up on her stomach and kneaded her claws. At once, she thought of John and the empty feeling she'd fallen asleep with came back in spades. With the soft mewing of her kittens, the cat jumped off the couch, leaving Megan drowsy, half asleep and consumed with thoughts of John.

How she had yearned to respond to that wild kiss on the deck. His face had been damp and warm and his arms so incredibly strong. She had wanted to stay in his embrace for the rest of her life, but instead, anger had surfaced and she'd forced herself away from him.

Being in love was hell. If she'd known John before Robert, she would have understood the difference between thinking you were in love and knowing you were in love. She would have been able to see Robert for what he was. She would have been able to see that her mother was pushing. She would have been able to turn away from someone so stunningly wrong for her that it boggled the imagination!

But she hadn't, and now John couldn't seem to get past it. She suspected he was falling in love with her—why else would he have overreacted so when he'd seen her with Robert? She wasn't sure if he knew how to love, if he trusted his feelings, if he ever listened to his head and not the distant call of a past she wished she could seal in a barrel and sink to the bottom of the ocean. She was almost positive that, romantic notions aside, love wasn't enough. She kept thinking about those huge words...she was determined to never again underestimate their importance.

A thumping noise chased more thoughts from her brain and she sat up abruptly in the dark. Fully awake now, she finally realized it shouldn't be dark; the dock lights should be illuminating the cabin as they had when she'd fallen asleep. Thoughts of a power outage came and went in a blink as she further realized that despite the fact that there was no sound or vibration from an engine or the slap of the paddle, the boat was moving. In a stomach-wrenching moment, she knew that the boat was adrift. The thumping came again.

Her cabin lights worked, thank goodness. She was already dressed in her jeans and sweater, but she took a moment to put on the deck shoes before tearing open her door and running down to the main deck.

What greeted her eyes stunned her into inactivity for a second. The stern-wheeler was traveling rapidly downriver. Shore lights illuminated the reckless passage as the big boat careered through the water along with trees and logs so massive and so plentiful it was a wonder they didn't crack the boat into a thousand pieces.

The deep thump came again and she ran to the side. The stern line was still tied to part of the pier being dragged alongside the boat. Every once in a while, it would slam against the hull. She immediately thought of the wicked-looking fire ax affixed to the wheelhouse door and went to get it. It took three or four chops, but finally the line split and the pier disappeared behind her.

She was too numb to address her fear. Her mind worked in an orderly fashion that now told her it was time to stop this boat from going any further downriver. But how? She thought of the wheelhouse and ran back up the stairs.

The lights flicked on but they were dim and she remembered they were running off a battery and not the generator. For a second she wondered if she could start the twin generators located in the engine room three decks below her—it was the only way to start the paddle working, which was the only way to propel and maneuver the boat. This would have to be done from the wheelhouse. She knew this because Norm used to recite the facts to his passengers every day, but the knowledge presently seemed almost worse than worthless.

The radio!

She switched on all the electronic equipment, one after the other. Not a single light blinked, nothing beeped. They were all dead.

Stop the boat, stop the boat... her mind frantically raced. She thought of the anchor.

Leaving the wheelhouse, she ran back across the deck and went two decks down, then headed back to the bow.

Oh, John, please, come...

For an instant she recalled the irritation she'd felt with him for trying to save her from Robert and his lawyer, and here she was praying for him to save her from the river. How was a man supposed to know from which things a woman needed saving?

"She'd have to tell him," Megan said, gasping as she slipped and ran into an iron bulkhead. She almost saw stars as she gripped her head with one hand, already feeling the swelling under her fingers.

"No time for this," she muttered as she finally reached the bow and the anchor windlass that Danny had fooled around with on a day not so long ago. It was topped with what looked like a metal steering wheel with a handle attached.

Danny had cranked it to the right.

So, crank it to the left.

It wouldn't budge. She finally noticed she was still holding the ax and, swinging it like a longshoreman, she banged the handle, once, twice, three times.

It moved. Immediately her ears were filled with the rattle of the anchor line playing out of the locker below, running across the windlass, disappearing through the hull fitting. A plop in the river announced the anchor had hit

the water, but the chain kept coming and she wasn't sure
how to stop it.

*Well, if a little chain is good, maybe a lot of chain is
better.*

Freed of action for a moment, she looked out at the river
and found that this close to the water, the view was truly
terrifying. As daylight approached, she could see the dark
shapes of huge logs and pieces of buildings, oil drums and
small boats, even a wayward hot tub. She could feel the
reverberation of the hull when things slammed against the
ship. The shore seemed way too close. They were past the
industrial part of town she was familiar with from their
excursions, headed toward Astoria and the Pacific ocean,
and still the line played out. She crossed every digit she
possessed in the fervent hope that the anchor would catch
on the bottom of the river and halt this horrible trip before
the boat crashed to shore and destroyed itself...and her.

The end of the line came with a jerk. For a second she
thought it had caught, and she gasped out a cry of relief,
but the second passed and the boat kept moving. Megan
sank down to the deck, cradling her throbbing head, heedless of the blood seeping into her hair. She thought of the
generators. It was the only thing left to try.

Oh, John....

Chapter Eleven

John gunned the truck, spinning out as he hit a water slick. The metal gates he was aiming for stood ajar, and he careered through them, coming to a stop beside a tiny office. Leaving Lily in the truck, he was out in a flash, pounding on the door. No one answered and the door was locked.

"Hey, you!" he heard.

He spun around. A flashlight blinded him so that he couldn't make out the identity of the person holding it. He threw his arm up to protect his vision.

"What do you think you're doing?"

"I need help," John gasped. "A boat—"

"Is that you, Vermont?" a man asked.

"Put down the light. Yes, it's me."

The light lowered and John saw he was looking at Benton Yates, the guy he'd sold his tugboat company to years before.

"I was just checking lines... What in the blazes are you doing down here in this mess?" Yates demanded.

John crossed to Benton's side immediately. In short, terse sentences he told how the pier had torn loose of the

piling, taking the *Ruby Rose* and at least one person downriver. "I need a boat," he said.

"The coast guard—"

"I haven't had time to call them. Give me a boat,
Yates."

"I've got them piled three deep. The one on the outside
is the thirty-foot launch—"

John was already jumping onto the deck of the first tug.
He heard Yates following him. He leaped to the second
boat and crossed it, then climbed down to the smaller boat.

"Untie me," he yelled up at Yates.

"Hell, I'm going with you," Yates hollered back and,
climbing aboard, untied the lines while John started the
diesel engine.

They turned on the searchlight, which illuminated a wild
brown river littered with debris. John switched on the radar
as Yates took over the steering.

Nothing. "I'll do lookout on the bow, you keep an eye
on the screen," John shouted over the noise of the diesel
engines.

The bow was open. Spray stung John's face as they
charged downriver. He knew how lucky he was to have
run across Yates, that there wasn't a more fearless man on
the river unless it was him. Yates was pushing the limits
out of concern for a boat and a life. John felt as though
he was literally racing to save two lives—Megan's, and in
a sense, his own.

He shouldn't have left her alone on the boat. His senses
had been so fogged with the knowledge that he was losing
Megan that he'd ignored all the signs that something like
this was bound to occur. If anything happened to her...

"There's something big about three miles downriver,"
Yates yelled at last.

John nodded. Dawn was coming, casting short rays of
light on a surreal scene. The river was so high that the
shoreline had completely changed. They were down a lot

farther than he went on everyday business. He saw houses awash, livestock stranded on islands of higher ground, people rowing across flooded fields. He could only imagine the scope of the damage and the rescue attempts that would be made during the course of this day. His own mind was consumed with the rescue of Megan Ashley Morison.

And then he saw her. The *Ruby Rose*. A big, old, gaudy boat looking totally out of place, right smack in the middle of the river. He tried to figure out if she was moving and sighed with relief when he saw she was getting bigger and bigger as they drew closer. At the very least, they were gaining ground. He made his way back to Yates.

Yates wordlessly handed him a pair of binoculars.

Peering through the glasses, John said, "Looks like she's got an anchor line out."

"Lucky for you there was someone aboard."

John couldn't respond. There was a knot the size of a cantaloupe in his throat. The ship looked okay, but he could find no sign of Megan.

"Think the hook will hold?"

He worked the cantaloupe away by swallowing. "She'll hold."

"Then we can go back and get one of the bigger tugs," Yates said, slowing down as they drew opposite the sternwheeler. "I'll tow you back to my dock."

John was shaking his head. "Can you get close to her?"

"I suppose. Why?"

"I want to go aboard. You're going to have your hands filled today, Benton, with people who need you a whole lot more than I do. I'll go aboard, make sure my... crew...is safe, check the hook and wait this out."

Benton stared at him a second. "You sure you want to do it this way?"

"Oh, yes," he said.

Yates nodded curtly.

"And Lily, my dog, she's inside the truck. You'll have to get her out of there. She knows her way around a tug."

"I remember," Yates said with a smile. "Sure, I'll take good care of her for you."

"Thanks, pal," John said sincerely.

"Don't get mushy on me," Yates snapped.

With expert skill, he brought the launch so close it was dwarfed by the stern-wheeler. John waited until the boats were close to touching and quickly stepped from the deck of one to the railing of the other, which he leaped over quickly, landing with both feet on the lower deck of the *Ruby Rose.*

"I'll stand by," Yates hollered.

John quickly made his way to the bow. Here he found all the anchor chain played out. He took care of making sure the *Ruby Rose* didn't go anywhere, then waved Yates off.

That's when he finally noticed the ax on the deck—and the blood. His heart froze.

Yates was gone. It was too late to call him back.

Well, if he needed help getting Megan to the hospital, he could use the radio to call the coast guard and if it was minor—please, please, let it be minor—he could launch the skiff. He began searching the ship.

Megan, holding an ice bag against her head, saw the launch as it was leaving. The anchor had bit just seconds before she was going to start the generators. She'd watched it for a while, marking her place on the river by lining up a barn on shore—or what had once been shore. Assured that the boat was safe, she'd buried herself in the galley, digging ice out of the freezer and sealing it in a plastic bag. It wasn't until she'd climbed back to the top deck that she saw the boat speeding away. She hollered and waved her arms to no avail.

All this action made her head throb again, and she decided to go up to her office to find aspirin.

She had just stepped on the first stair when she heard a voice—no, not just a voice, John's wonderful, beloved voice! She turned as he reached the top of the stairs and saw her. The look on his face had to mirror the look on her face and for some seconds, they stared at each other with stunned disbelief.

John, tears springing to his eyes at the sight of Megan's beautiful—and safe—face, began moving toward her. It was decision time. Did he want to live in his past, eaten alive with distrust, alone and miserable? Or did he want to embrace the woman in front of him, a woman who had dared to use the word *love*, embrace her as his future, trust her and return her love, be faithful to her, make her his wife, adore her forever and ever?

There wasn't a doubt in his mind.

They stopped a foot short of touching.

"You hurt your head," he said.

"It doesn't hurt anymore," she said, dropping the ice bag.

"Megan, I thought you were gone," he said, reaching out to smooth her tousled hair from her eyes.

She leaned into his hand and smiled. *This* was the smile, he realized with a start. *This* was a smile for him, a true smile, a smile of a woman who knows what she wants—and whom.

"I saved your ship," she said softly.

"I know. Thank you."

"So, can't I claim salvage rights?"

"I don't know," he said, stroking her cheek.

"I'll get a lawyer."

He reached out with his other hand and caught her around the waist, pulling her against him. She came willingly. He took a second to part her hair and check the laceration, which wasn't so bad after all, then he tilted her chin and gazed into her eyes.

"You don't need a lawyer," he said. "I'll give her to you."

"Thank you. I love her, you know."

"Yes, I know."

"The radio was broken... All the electronic whiz-a-gigs didn't work."

"There's a master switch," he said, kissing her forehead, reveling in the taste of her.

She pulled back a couple of inches. "John, I was terrified."

"Oh, my darling," he said, once again embracing her. "So was I."

"But I did it. I stopped this old boat from planting itself in the middle of a field. I think I'm a lot more capable than I ever gave myself credit for."

"No kidding," he whispered.

"I didn't want you to lose your boat."

"I didn't want to lose you," he said.

She smiled, her dimples impish and adorable, and he was forced to kiss her. As always, the fresh taste of her hinted at an underlying sensuality that completely possessed him.

"I love you," he said at last. "I have since the moment I saw you standing here getting ready to marry the wrong guy. And you were right, I was so sure you were another Betsy that I didn't realize you were Meg. Megan. My Megan."

"Meg is okay," she said. "I like it when you call me that."

"I misjudged you continually. I was afraid to admit how important you were becoming to me, how perfect a woman you were for a man like me. I was looking at you as though you were a cracked plate."

She wrinkled her forehead. "A cracked plate?"

"It doesn't matter," he said. "What I'm trying to tell you is, Megan, I'm sorry. I want you to forgive me. I'm asking for you to forgive me."

She lowered her eyes. "I was a mess when you met me, John. In the space of a few weeks, I've learned more about life and myself than I did in all the years that came before. I threw you curve balls without meaning to. I sent mixed signals." Meeting his gaze again, she added, "I'm sorry."

"You haven't told me yet," he said.

"Told you what?"

"If you love me, too. If it's not too late for us."

She smiled that secret smile that just about drove him insane. "I have standards," she said. "I want to have children and they'll need a father who not only loves them, but who likes them."

"Do-able," he said.

"I need to be trusted and I need to trust."

"Absolutely."

"I need a promise of forever by a man who isn't sour on the idea of marriage."

"Who, me?"

"And I need someplace on this boat to sell those damn disposable cameras."

"You're the captain," he said. "You can sell them anyplace your heart desires."

She cupped his face in both her hands. "Then the answer, my recalcitrant darling, is yes, I love you. I have since I first saw you, standing here in your uniform, your eyes so blue they penetrated me, your strength so tangible I could feel it. I've loved you since the moment before I said 'I do' to the wrong man. And now I love you for all the right reasons…your humor, your heart, the way you love me."

John picked her up in his arms and slowly twirled her around. There was just the two of them, stuck on a huge boat with days of food and drink aboard, out in the sunlight while the flooded world surrounded but didn't touch them. It was a time out of time, a place out of place. She held on to his neck and beamed at him until he claimed her mouth and made her each and every promise she'd asked for and then some.

He whispered, "Will you marry me?"

Without pause or hesitation or any trace of doubt, she said, "Of course."

A sense of peace descended on him. A rich, wonderful feeling of wholeness. "We never had our dance," he finally managed to say.

"What's wrong with now?"

He put her down, opened his arms and felt as though he'd just captured the world as she came to him. Neither one of them paid the slightest attention to the helicopter passing overhead.

In the days and weeks to come, when the television news aired a montage of the flood entitled "FLOOD!" they caught sight of themselves dancing on the open deck, wrapped in each other's arms, caught by a Channel 9 television crew out surveying the damage. This image played and replayed, all over the country, heralded as a triumph of the human spirit in the midst of a major disaster.

And on these occasions, John Vermont would exchange a smile and a look of pure adoration with his new wife, who was invariably nuzzling a small gray kitten while a large yellow dog watched. And he would think to himself, if they only knew the half of it!

* * * * *

Maternity Leave

Coming September 1998

Three delightful stories about the blessings and surprises of "Labor" Day.

TABLOID BABY by Candace Camp

She was whisked to the hospital in the nick of time....

THE NINE-MONTH KNIGHT
by Cait London

A down-on-her-luck secretary is experiencing odd little midnight cravings....

THE PATERNITY TEST by Sherryl Woods

The stick turned blue before her biological clock struck twelve....

These three special women are very pregnant...and very single, although they won't be either for too much longer, because baby—and Daddy—are on their way!

Available at your favorite retail outlet.

Look us up on-line at: http://www.romance.net   PSMATLEV

Take 2 bestselling love stories FREE

Plus get a FREE surprise gift!

Special Limited-Time Offer

Mail to Silhouette Reader Service™

3010 Walden Avenue
P.O. Box 1867
Buffalo, N.Y. 14240-1867

YES! Please send me 2 free Silhouette Romance™ novels and my free surprise gift. Then send me 6 brand-new novels every month, which I will receive months before they appear in bookstores. Bill me at the low price of $2.90 each plus 25¢ delivery and applicable sales tax, if any.* That's the complete price, and a saving of over 10% off the cover prices—quite a bargain! I understand that accepting the books and gift places me under no obligation ever to buy any books. I can always return a shipment and cancel at any time. Even if I never buy another book from Silhouette, the 2 free books and the surprise gift are mine to keep forever.

215 SEN CH7S

Name	(PLEASE PRINT)
Address	Apt. No.
City	State	Zip

This offer is limited to one order per household and not valid to present Silhouette Romance™ subscribers. *Terms and prices are subject to change without notice. Sales tax applicable in N.Y.

USROM-98   ©1990 Harlequin Enterprises Limited

International bestselling author

JOAN JOHNSTON

continues her wildly popular Hawk's Way miniseries with an all-new, longer-length novel

THE SUBSTITUTE GROOM

HAWK'S WAY

August 1998

Jennifer Wright's hopes and dreams had rested on her summer wedding—until a single moment changed everything. Including the *groom*. Suddenly Jennifer agreed to marry her fiancé's best friend, a darkly handsome Texan she needed—and desperately wanted—almost against her will. But U.S. Air Force Major Colt Whitelaw had sacrificed too much to settle for a marriage of convenience, and that made hiding her passion all the more difficult. And hiding her biggest secret downright impossible...

"Joan Johnston does contemporary Westerns to perfection." —*Publishers Weekly*

Available in August 1998
wherever Silhouette books are sold.

Look us up on-line at: http://www.romance.net

PSHWKWAY

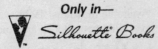